MONTVILLE TOWNSHIP PUBLIC LIBRARY
W9-BYU-066
3

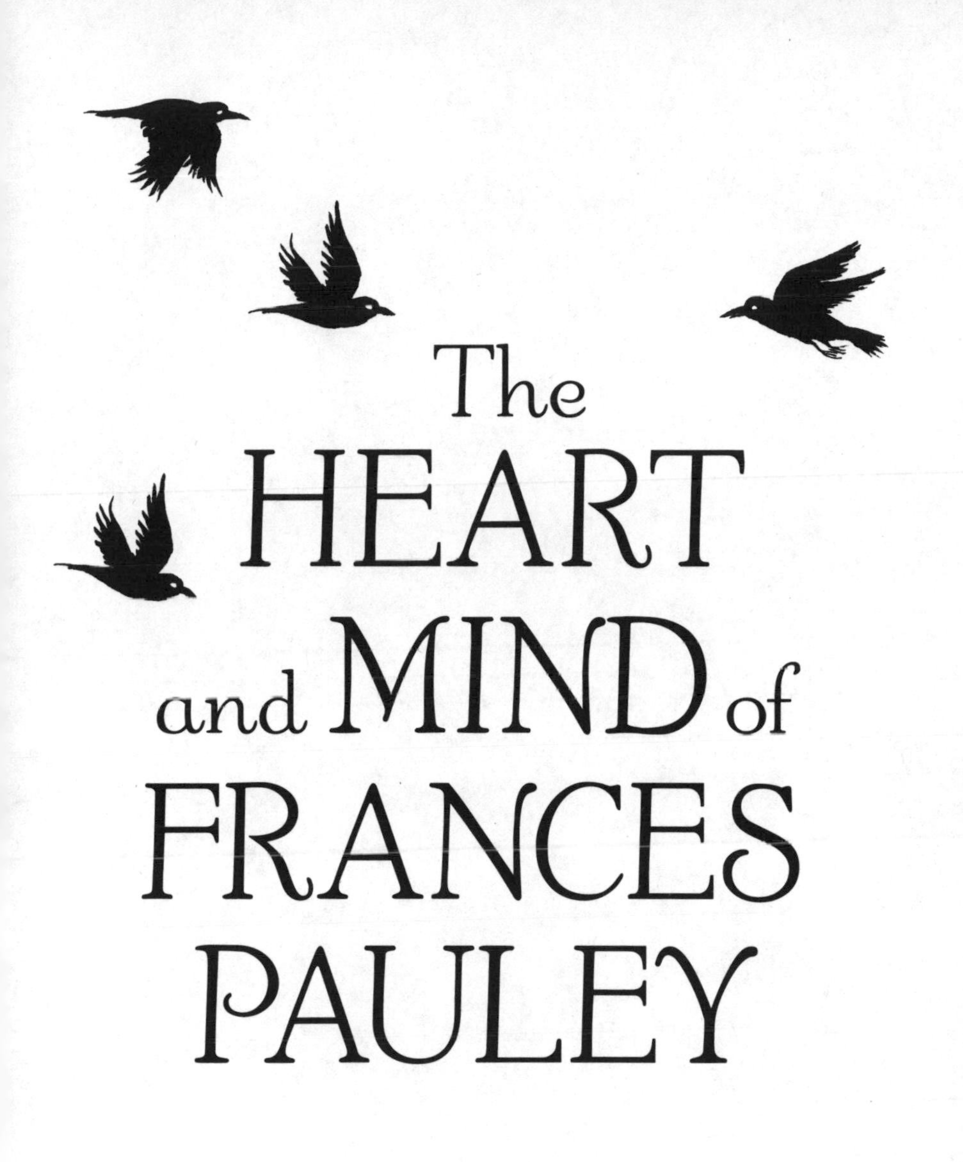

The HEART and MIND of FRANCES PAULEY

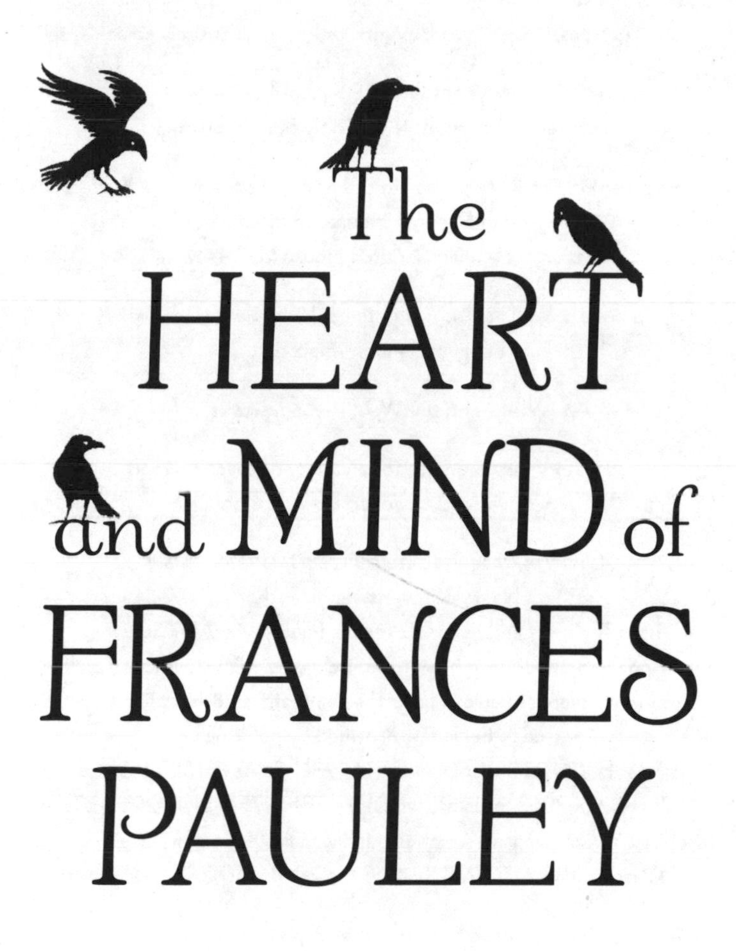

by APRIL STEVENS

schwartz & wade books • new york

 Published in the United States by Schwartz & Wade Books, an imprint of Random House Children's Books, a division of Penguin Random House LLC, New York.

Schwartz & Wade Books and the colophon are trademarks of Penguin Random House LLC.

Visit us on the Web! rhcbooks.com

Educators and librarians, for a variety of teaching tools, visit us at RHTeachersLibrarians.com

Library of Congress Cataloging-in-Publication Data
Names: Stevens, April, author.
Title: The heart and mind of Frances Pauley / by April Stevens.
Description: First edition. | New York : Schwartz & Wade Books, [2018] |
Summary: "Frances Pauley learns the value of friendship while staying true to herself"—Provided by publisher.
Identifiers: LCCN 2017006817 | ISBN 978-1-5247-2061-2 (hardcover) |
ISBN 978-1-5247-2062-9 (library binding) | ISBN 978-1-5247-2063-6 (ebook)
Subjects: | CYAC: Friendship—Fiction. | Individuality—Fiction. | Death—Fiction.
Classification: LCC PZ7.S84315 He 2018 | DDC [Fic]—dc23

The text of this book is set in 13-point Garamond.
Book design by Rachael Cole

Printed in the United States of America
2 4 6 8 10 9 7 5 3 1
First Edition

For Sam and Willa

PART ONE

CHAPTER ONE

Unlike her sister, Figgrotten went right outside after school and climbed the rocks behind their house and looked for things. Mostly birds, but bugs and different stones too. She had made herself a kind of room up on the rocks. It had sticks around it for walls and a built-in rock-chair that had moss growing on it, and it had a dent that sometimes, after it rained, served as a nice sink.

Figgrotten's sister, Christinia, on the other hand, would go straight to her bedroom and make her bed and put away all her clothes and dust her furniture, then put on sappy music and stare at herself in the mirror. She had long hair that she kept perfect and pinned.

Figgrotten did not even try to manage her own hair, as it was not that kind of hair. It felt like dry grass, and after a bad experience with a burr once, she kept it shorter and most often wore a hat. It was one of those hats with the earflaps that hung down. She wore it not only to cover her hair but also because when she wore it she felt snappier. Christinia found the hat an embarrassment, and this seemed to be another reason Figgrotten liked to wear it. She'd discovered that the more Christinia hated certain things about her, the more she clung to those things in defiance.

Her best friend in the whole world, Alvin Turkson, was always saying, "People have to accept each other or wars break out." But Christinia was the opposite of accepting, in fact, she seemed downright intolerant of Figgrotten these days. At night, when her sister would strum her guitar in her bedroom next door and sing in her beautiful voice, Figgrotten's heart would get tugged at and a loneliness would come over her. She would have liked to go in and sit with Christinia and tell her she loved her singing, but now she knew to keep her distance.

CHAPTER TWO

Figgrotten had been going up to her rocks for years. It was where she felt most herself. Sometimes she was out there until after dark and Christinia would come out on the back lawn and say the word "dinner" in a sour, disgusted voice and Figgrotten would climb down and go back inside. The fact was, she hated being inside. She felt like she couldn't breathe indoors. Especially at dinnertime, when she was made to take off her hat and wash her hands and eat in the stuffy kitchen.

Often, at dinner, she'd ask questions that seemed to confuse her family. Things like "I read that Margaret

Mead used to just hang up the phone when she was done talking to people. She didn't even say goodbye. Just *clunk,* put the receiver down. Do you think that was because the people she studied didn't have telephones?" Figgrotten really liked Margaret Mead, an anthropologist who had studied tribes of people living in the middle of nowhere without telephones or toilets. The thing that had drawn Figgrotten to her to begin with was a photograph she'd found of Margaret Mead in the World Book Encyclopedia. She looked a bit strident, wore a cape and a hat, and carried a walking stick. At first Figgrotten even thought her face looked kind of manly. She stared at the picture for quite a while. Then she started reading about Margaret Mead's life and found it super interesting.

She'd never even heard of anthropology before this, but once she did, she thought it might be something she might like to do when she grew up. Mostly because it involved a lot of outdoor work. One thing Figgrotten knew for sure was that if she had to work inside somewhere, she'd probably suffocate. But the other thing that she liked about anthropology was that it involved observing people, and Figgrotten was a natural observer. She observed birds and trees and clouds and, once she stopped to think about it, she did lots of observing of people too. Her sister, of course, being one of those people. Not because she found Christinia all that interesting, but more because she was trying to figure out exactly what made her tick.

Figgrotten kept her bedroom windows open at night, and she'd brought a lot of branches up there so that it felt kind of woodsy. Initially this exasperated her mother, but now her mom didn't go into her room as much. She told Figgrotten that she just couldn't take the mess. At first Figgrotten wasn't sure what to make of her victory, but soon she came around to it. Not having her mom come in there all the time and yell at her about all the leaves and sticks actually made life in the house calmer.

Due to the open windows, Figgrotten's room would get super cold in the winter, which was how she liked it. She slept in her wool hat and socks, and sometimes, when it was really blowing in there, she wore her wool coat to bed. She'd bundle up and lie stiff as a board and breathe in the cold clear air. She loved it! Loved the way the air hit the back of her throat, startling her a little each time.

Back when Christinia was still talking to Figgrotten, Christinia would go into Figgrotten's room and just about go berserk. She'd beat at the branches and get all crazy that the place was so untidy.

"What is the matter with you?" she once shrieked. "Why can't you be normal? And why do you have that stupid name pinned to your door? That's just so weird!"

Christinia was referring to the name *Figgrotten,* which Figgrotten had given to herself a few years ago, writing it out in her then-crooked handwriting and tacking it on her door. Her real name was Frances Pauley, which she felt didn't suit her, so she put all sorts of words together, backward and forward. Once "fig" and "rotten" rolled off her tongue together that first time, it stuck. And from then on she thought of herself not as Frances but as Figgrotten, adding the extra *g* because that's the growly way it sounded to her. Giving herself this name felt strangely freeing. It allowed her to be able to just be herself more. Not Frances. But Figgrotten.

Figgrotten thought it was a dumb way to live, feeling like everything had to be the way *you* thought it should be or you'd just freak out. So she'd finally said to Christinia, "What makes you think *you're* so normal? And what makes you the expert on what normal even is?" which made her sister's mouth drop open at first before tears came into her eyes and she burst out through the branches, slamming the door behind her. It obviously had never occurred to Christinia before that *normal* might not be the same thing for everyone. Though Figgrotten knew what she'd meant and Christinia *was* more typical than she was. Anyway, that was the last time Christinia had been in Figgrotten's room, and that had happened right before school started. Then there had been another incident in the auditorium soon after that, in September, that seemed to make things worse.

Now, in January, they pretty much never talked. Just the sight of Figgrotten seemed to infuriate Christinia and make her look sickened. So there seemed no choice but to give Christinia a super wide berth and avoid her at all costs. It wasn't what Figgrotten would have wanted. They used to have fun together. Sometimes they would make things to eat in the kitchen. Brownie pies and little pizzas on toast. Back when they were younger, Figgrotten and Christinia would watch cartoons on Sunday mornings and play I Spy in the backseat of the car when they went places. Figgrotten definitely missed those times, but she somehow knew something about Christinia had changed, and this change made Figgrotten feel uneasy. Come to think of it, she didn't quite even know who Christinia was anymore.

At least Figgrotten got along nicely with her parents.

The reason for this, mostly, was that she was an excellent student and she also did her chores like they were going out of style. She loved doing chores, actually. She enjoyed checking things off a to-do list. Garbage taken out, clothes folded, cat fed. So, other than her devotion to the out-of-doors and the condition of her room, her parents didn't have a whole lot to complain about. She was the best student in her class and she liked homework as well and did all of it up on the rocks each afternoon. She first did her math, which she liked the least; then she did her reading and poetry and vocabulary words. Then, as a kind of dessert, she'd read the encyclopedia.

She'd never even heard of encyclopedias before she found a whole set of World Book volumes down in her dad's office in the basement of their house. He'd had them from when he was a kid and then never had the heart to chuck them all out. Once Figgrotten got her hands on one, she knew why he'd kept them. They were impossible to put down. The color photos, the short paragraphs about absolutely everything. While she could have sat down at the family's big computer in the living room and probably found all this stuff, having the books to hold while she was up on the rocks made them especially perfect. Plus, when she looked online, there was too much information for her to sort through. In a book it was more pared down and not so overwhelming.

At the moment, she was pawing through the *C*'s, though she didn't go through the books in order, and had just gulped down two fascinating paragraphs about crows. Not everything gripped her, but crows were interesting. She'd always known, from being up on the rocks and being surrounded by them, that they were not your average sort of bird. They didn't just go about their business. They had a complex life up in the trees and spent half their time screaming and yelling at cach other. Sometimes, Figgrotten had observed, they went absolutely bananas, and if she spent a little time looking around she could usually figure out what it was that was getting them all flustered. Sometimes it was a hawk, circling up above. Sometimes it was Figgrotten's cat, Clark, sitting out on the back porch cleaning his paws. Anyway, crows, Figgrotten learned, were birds with an above-average intelligence. Not unlike herself. Perhaps this was why she felt a kinship to them.

At the beginning of the school year, in September, her fifth-grade teacher, Mr. Stanley, hadn't been sure what to make of Figgrotten. He told her parents that for such a clever girl she rarely contributed to class discussions and sometimes he caught her staring out the window. But Figgrotten had her reasons for this, and once she was able to explain, she and Mr. Stanley became friends. She didn't like to talk too much in class because she found when she did the other kids became sort of lumpy and sullen.

She'd discovered this in first grade when the teacher had gotten on the subject of dinosaurs and she became so excited that she would raise her hand to the point where she lifted straight out of her seat, all while making little oohing noises. She pretty much took over each class with her questions and hand-raising, until finally she noticed that each time her hand went up, most of her classmates sank down in their seats and some even looked like they were going to be sick. The fact was, she started to figure out they hadn't a clue half the time what she was even talking about. So, once she saw that she was being annoying, she quieted herself down. And now, sometimes, she had to admit she was a little bored because of this, and the only way she could combat the boredom was to look out the window at the sky and think.

"An improper fraction. Anyone, anyone?" Mr. Stanley would be up at the front of the classroom, and

Figgrotten would have two layers of thoughts. One was about fractions and the other was simply *How incredible that there's a moon up there in the sky in the middle of the day.*

"Frances." Mr. Stanley would walk over to Figgrotten and touch her shoulder. "An improper fraction?"

"It's a fraction that has a top number that is larger than the bottom number," Figgrotten would answer, trying not to sound unwilling but feeling everyone slump down a little. It was sort of awful, but she couldn't pretend she didn't know. That would be just plain ridiculous. She knew that lots of the kids in her class had sharp minds, but for some reason they didn't use them the way they should. It just didn't make sense to her. Being a thinker wasn't something you needed to hide. It was just something, Figgrotten had learned, you didn't necessarily want to flaunt.

Figgrotten's favorite time of day, like everyone else's, was recess. She would burst through the doors, out of the overheated and stuffy classroom, and gulp in fresh air. The playground was a fenced-in area with a jungle gym and swings and a basketball court. The crazy thing was that the woods were right out past the fence, and of course that was where the playground should have started. Out there in the woods was where kids could actually have some fun. In fact, Figgrotten had written Mr. Stanley a letter about this earlier in the year.

> Mr. Stanley,
>
> I think our playground would be better if part of the woods were fenced in too. That way kids could be out in nature during recess and there is a lot more to learn in the woods than on mowed grass and pavement.
>
> Frances

Mr. Stanley had written back to her.

> Dear Frances,
>
> You have made a valid point. I will bring this up with Mrs. Flynn and get back to you.
>
> Sincerely,
>
> Mr. Stanley

But nothing came of any of it. Figgrotten was told a week later that Mrs. Flynn, the principal, said that to refence the playground would cost too much money, and also the woods were not "to code" and were filled with things that could be dangerous. Sticks that could poke into eyes and insects that could crawl up pant legs. Figgrotten noticed when Mr. Stanley reported this to her that his mouth tightened up a bit and moved slightly to one side of his face. It seemed he was holding back from grimacing. She could only take this to mean he too was not happy with Mrs. Flynn's boring way of thinking. Figgrotten let it go at that. But it bothered her. Being boring bothered her just about more than anything.

However, despite all this, recess remained her most stimulating period at school, as she liked to tell anyone who asked. Even within the chain-link fence, nature prevailed. There were a few little shrubs around, and under the shrubs, in the moist earth, interesting things could be found. Spider eggs and worms and, of course, bugs. Bugs were everywhere if you spent two seconds looking for them. Figgrotten gave herself the task of finding and identifying one bug, one worm, and one bird during each recess. She brought out her notebook with her lists and drawings and got right to work. Often, whether she wanted company or not, she'd be joined by one or two kids. In general, kids tended to be curious. They were like cats in that way. Whether they wanted to admit it or not, they always wanted to know what was going on. And most often, with Figgrotten, something was going on. She'd be down on her hands and knees under a forsythia bush and she'd be muttering, "Holy moly, what the devil is that?"

"What? What? What is it?"

"I think it's a bug with a kind of horn on its head. Kind of like a rhino."

And before long there'd be twenty kids pushing to check it out while Figgrotten drew a picture of it and wrote "Bug with rhino horn" for later identification and then stood up and dusted herself off.

She felt exhilarated after such finds and could only imagine what it must have been like for people who really, truly discovered things. For instance, Donald Johanson, the guy who found Lucy, the four-million-year-old skeleton, must have just about jumped out of his underwear when he dug *her* up.

Figgrotten had a poster of Lucy up in her room. Christinia had gone insane when Figgrotten had taped it to her wall back when she was in second grade. "You can't have a picture of some skeleton on your wall! What if someone sees it? That is just plain creepy and weird!"

"It's not just *some* skeleton," she'd told Christinia,

who definitely was not listening. "She's the oldest person ever. It's not creepy at all. She's a relative of ours."

And that was how she viewed it. She viewed the laid-out bones lovingly, almost as if this was a friend of hers. Lucy. What a wonderful name for this little person. Figgrotten would lie in her bed and gaze at the poster.

There were several hundred pieces of her bones they found when they discovered her. Several hundred!

In the afternoons, after she got off the school bus, Figgrotten would walk straight into the kitchen with her jacket and backpack on, grab a handful of cookies or a granola bar, then go straight out the back door and up onto the rocks. The Pauleys' house didn't have much of a real yard. It was backed right into a kind of cliff of steep jagged rocks. Figgrotten's rock room was about halfway up on a nice big ledge; then behind that the rocks went up farther, and at the top there were the towering pine trees and the woods. To get up to her room, she climbed the natural steps that zigzagged her right up to the ledge. Then, if she wanted to go up even farther, there were more steps, but these were the ones that made her mom nervous, so she didn't venture up there too often.

She had a routine once she got up to her rock room. First she'd sit down and close her eyes for a few seconds and listen. It was almost better than seeing. If she just listened, she could quickly figure out where the birds were: She could hear their wings fluttering in the branches up above her. Or hear them chattering. And she could hear if there was any animal hopping around in the woods.

After she opened her eyes, when the weather was warmer, she would look around at her feet for bugs, and if she saw one, she would follow it for a while. But often she had to stop in the middle of her bug tracking, pull out her math, and get to work.

Sometimes while she was doing her work she'd glance down at the house. She could see into the kitchen, where her mom often stood making dinner. She could see the light on through the tiny basement window and she'd know her dad was down there in his office, where he worked on people's taxes. But worst of all, she could see into Christinia's bedroom window from a certain angle and sometimes she could see her sister in there. Once, unfortunately, she'd even seen her in her bra, standing sideways and looking in the mirror.

So that afternoon in early January when she happened to glance through Christinia's window and saw her sister lying facedown on her bed sobbing, it made her wish she wasn't quite so observant. But once she saw Christinia, she found she couldn't forget it. She craned her neck and leaned down farther for a better view and now saw that Christinia's shoulders were heaving up and down.

Figgrotten looked away. She whistled a bit under her breath and went back to her math pages, but after another minute or two she found that she was looking again. Christinia hadn't moved. She was still lying there, her face planted into her pillow. Figgrotten went back to her work but her mind was fumbly. What would make Christinia cry like that? Of course, had Christinia known Figgrotten had seen her, she would have ripped Figgrotten's eyeballs clean out of her head. Figgrotten pulled her hat down and leaned harder into her work, using her mind like the beam of a flashlight and directing it only on the fraction at hand, trying hard to block out all her questions, not to mention the ache of sadness in her chest for her sister.

CHAPTER THREE

Figgrotten sat in the front seat of the school bus every single day on her way to school and on her way home. Not only did she get a nice blast of cold air each time the door was opened, but, more importantly, Alvin Turkson was the bus driver and Figgrotten was seated directly behind him.

Alvin was different from any other grown-up, and at times she didn't even view him as one. He was just her friend. The only person who Figgrotten felt really understood her. The truth was, he was like that with all the kids, respectful of their true natures. Even the worst ones, who sat in the last seat and burped loudly and threw wadded-up pieces of paper into the backs of other kids' heads, even those he never became angry with. Sometimes he would tell someone they had beans in their jeans, but that was about it.

Alvin was about a hundred years old and smaller than most of the eighth graders, and ever since she had known him he had worn the same black Greek fisherman's hat, which had a worn-down look to it. But the thing that set him apart more than anything was that he was curious about everything. He wanted to know what Figgrotten had eaten for breakfast. He wanted to know what kind of music Christinia liked to play on her guitar. He wanted to know what birds Figgrotten could hear up in what he called her "rock world."

"Now, don't forget all those warblers in the springtime," he would tell her. "Once you start being able to identify the warbler calls, well, then you're a serious birder."

The morning after Figgrotten spied her sister crying in her room, Alvin, who seemed to have sharp instincts about what went on with people, said to Christinia when she climbed onto the bus behind Figgrotten, "Now, Miss Christinia, each day you get taller and prettier."

Figgrotten, who had plopped into the seat behind

Alvin, turned and saw her sister straighten up a little as she set off down the aisle.

"And you, Miss Pauley," Alvin said, looking at Figgrotten in the rearview mirror, "what thoughts are filling your mind today?"

"Um, not all that much. Mostly thoughts about crows," Figgrotten said, sliding forward and talking over his shoulder.

"Ah!" Alvin was wearing his bulky wool sweater, and he leaned over and pulled the door shut. He made his funny high-pitched laugh and threw the bus into gear and off they went.

Between the roar of the bus and the fact that he was so old and hard of hearing, Figgrotten had to lean a little forward and shout when she spoke to him. "I've been reading about them, Alvin. They marry each other and stay together for life."

Alvin shook his head. "Now, is that so?"

"And when one of them dies, they have a funeral and sit around the dead one and look at it, then they all fly away at once."

"Well, I'll be." Alvin rubbed at his jaw with one hand while the other hand gripped the large steering wheel. "Crows do that, do they?"

Figgrotten sat back in her seat and looked out the

window. They were passing the tall pointy houses that lined the main street of Preston. A few slumpy people, looking cold and hunched up, were making their way along the sidewalks. Figgrotten wanted to turn around and look at Christinia in the back of the bus, but she knew she couldn't have her sister see her do this. She was bothered by having seen Christinia crying and wanted to find out what was making her so miserable. If she waited long enough, she figured one of the wild kids would cause some ruckus back there and Figgrotten would have an excuse to turn around.

"I once raised a crow," Alvin said over his shoulder. "Found it as a baby out on our front porch one day. Screaming to beat the band. Named her Miriam. Though, to be honest, I never was sure if it was a girl or a boy. But she rode around for a couple of years on my shoulder."

"A couple of years! Really?" Figgrotten sat forward again. "What happened to her?"

"She flew off when she was ready."

"Oh, I guess that was good." Figgrotten sat back in her seat. Then she hollered, "But you must have been so sad when she flew away!"

"Not too sad; she stayed around the place for years.

She'd come down to the low branches for a visit every now and then."

Figgrotten smiled and looked out the window. She had on the thick brown wool coat she'd found at the thrift store in Millington three winters earlier. The sleeves were too short now, up above her wrists and leaving a good two inches of bare skin down to her mittens. But it was one of several things Figgrotten refused to part with. She'd formed an attachment to it. She imagined herself wearing it until there was nothing left but several brown threads.

She sat plucking cat hair off it now. She liked to hold Clark in her arms each morning before she left for school. He loved that, being cradled like a baby. But because of this, the brown coat was half white with cat fur.

A minute later, when Alvin began slowing the bus down in an unexpected place, Figgrotten slid forward on her seat again and craned her neck to look. She could see that up ahead, standing on the sidewalk with a woman who had to be his mother, was a kid she'd never seen before.

"We have a new passenger!" Alvin said loud enough for everyone on the bus to hear.

Alvin pulled up and pushed open the door and

everyone on the bus grew quiet. The boy's mother, looking nervous, touched the boy's shoulder and he stepped onto the bus.

"This is—" she began to shout up to Alvin.

"James! Yes, yes!" Alvin filled in for her. "Welcome, James. Climb aboard. I'm Alvin and you just call me Alvin." Alvin stuck out his hand and James shook it, though he was clearly distracted by the daunting prospect of walking down the aisle for the first time.

"For the first few rides, you have to sit up front," Alvin told him, which was unquestionably a relief to the kid. This was Alvin's rule for all new kids, instituted years ago, before Figgrotten had even started riding the bus. James took off his pack and sat down across the aisle from her. He was tall and thin with shaggy dark hair and glasses, and he had on a well-worn army jacket. He glanced over at Figgrotten, met her eye, and quickly looked away. Figgrotten figured that due to her hat and cat-hair-covered coat, she had given the poor kid his first scare. He then unzipped his backpack and withdrew a big book. He opened it up in his lap, then slumped forward and started reading. *Huh,* she thought as the bus pulled away from the curb. She rarely saw a kid reading a book like that.

Soon the kids in the back grew louder, and sure

enough, as Figgrotten had figured, after a minute or so someone made a loud howling noise in an attempt, obviously, to scare the new kid. Figgrotten decided to use this as an excuse and she turned around and looked back over all the faces. She had to look harder and longer than she would have liked before her eyes landed on Christinia, who was sitting alone, staring glumly out the window. She usually sat back there chatting with her friends Becky and Claire, but they were sitting together on the other side of the bus today. Figgrotten spun quickly back around, making sure Christinia didn't see her.

"Everyone." Mr. Stanley was standing at the head of the room. "Everyone, quiet down. I want to introduce James Barren to you all. He will be a new member of our class."

James stood next to him, looking about as humiliated as a person could possibly look. Figgrotten had a better view of him there, displayed like that in the front of the class. Everything seemed to hang from him a bit: his dark brown hair and his jacket and even his jeans. He wore black-rimmed glasses that looked a bit big for him, and through them, Figgrotten saw his eyes quickly scanning the room.

"James is going to sit here next to Jacob, and Jacob, you're going to be James's guide for today. You're to show him everything. Where the gym is, where the restrooms are, where we go out for recess. You know, the ropes."

"What ropes?" Jacob said.

"That's an expression," Figgrotten said gently, and everyone turned and looked at her. "Show someone the ropes means show them around."

"That's right," Mr. Stanley said. "Now, how about we move on. Let's talk today about the poem that I wrote up here on the board. Would anyone like to read this out loud?"

Figgrotten kept her hand down. She would have liked to read it aloud. She was good at reading; plus, she really loved poetry. But she'd already burst out with one comment and now she needed to give it a rest.

"Fiona," Mr. Stanley said. "Could you do that for us?"

Everyone turned to the back of the class and Fiona Peterson stood up. Fiona was one of the better students in the class but she was also one of the quietest, the kind of kid Figgrotten, when she was going over everyone in her grade, would completely forget about.

"'The Bird,'" Fiona began in a papery whisper that Figgrotten could barely hear. "'Wings like piano keys fluttering upward through green trembling leaves . . .'"

When she was done, she sat down quickly and slumped into her seat.

"Well," Mr. Stanley said, "how about the students who liked the poem raise their hands."

Figgrotten shot her hand up, then glanced around. Fiona's hand was up, along with two other girls' and James's. Everyone else just sat there.

"Okay, I would like to hear from the people who didn't like the poem. Let's start with Russell. Russell, what about the poem made you not like it?"

Figgrotten saw Russell Gracey sink lower in his seat and shrug. "I don't know. I just don't like poems," he said, and everyone giggled.

"That's okay." Mr. Stanley smiled. "But you have to try a bit harder. What about this particular poem did you not like?"

Russell scrunched his face up and did another big shrug. "Um, I guess I thought it was too kind of, I don't know, too flowery or something."

"Aha!" Mr. Stanley said. "Wonderful, Russell. It *was* sort of flowery. So, maybe you don't like poems that are flowery. I'm going to find you some poems that are the opposite of flowery and see if I can get you to like poetry."

This was an example of why Figgrotten liked Mr. Stanley. He allowed people to have opinions and he made room for those opinions. He didn't squelch anyone the way her teacher Mrs. Garcia did last year. If someone didn't give her the answer she was looking for, she would look around the room and say, "Anyone else?" which made no one ever want to risk putting their hand up.

"Okay," Mr. Stanley said. "Let's talk about what we liked about this poem. How about you, James? What was it that you felt was good about it?"

James sat up a little taller in his seat and without pausing to consider the question he quickly said, "I liked the piano because it made me think of the sound when you run your hand fast up the keys. So I sort of heard that sound while at the same time I was picturing the bird going up through the trees."

Now it was Figgrotten who sank a tiny bit in her seat. She watched a look of excitement go across Mr. Stanley's face.

"Oh, absolutely!" he exclaimed, clapping his hands together. "Good listening, James. I thought the same thing the first time I heard this poem."

She hadn't really thought about the piano keys that much, but now suddenly she wished she had.

That afternoon at recess Figgrotten asked Mr. Stanley if she could go to the library instead of outdoors. This was not easy for her, because, as always, she would have preferred to be outside.

"I am studying crows," Figgrotten told him. "So I was going to see if there are any books about them." She wanted to know, for instance, how you could tell the difference between males and females. She might be able to tell Alvin the answer.

Mr. Stanley, who was sitting at his desk, wrote Figgrotten a library pass and handed it to her.

"Frances," he said, looking up at her, "I was hoping that you might also look out for James a bit."

"Me?" Figgrotten said. "But I thought . . ."

"Well, I just think you might be helpful to him at some point; he's a good student too."

"Oh."

"He was languishing in the last school he was in. You know what that word means, right?"

"He was getting kind of droopy because he was sort of bored?" Figgrotten sure did know that feeling. She'd felt a bit that way in Mrs. Garcia's class last year.

"That's right. I think he was a bit lonely as well."

Figgrotten shrugged her shoulders. "Okay." Though she had zero idea how *she* could be of any kind of help to him. She already felt as if she wasn't sure she liked him.

She chose a cubicle in the library and put down her book bag. Then she went to the library's computer and looked up online what books were available, first searching for books about crows. There were none, so she looked for general bird books. There were several she found and lugged back to the cubicle, but there was little about crows in any of them that she didn't already know. A group of them was called a murder. She knew that. A murder of crows. There was always one crow who had the job of being lookout for the others. She knew that too. She sighed. She could have been outside in the fresh air.

As she was heading out of the library a few minutes later, a group of eighth-grade girls passed her. They were all falling in toward each other, stumbling together in a fit of loud crazy laughter. Figgrotten stepped aside to let them go by, but none of them noticed her. They were too caught up in their joke. She knew all of them. These were Christinia's friends. There was

Jessica Frankenhart and Becky Moss and Claire Halberstam and Amber Lurie. But why wasn't Christinia with them? Figgrotten felt mean suddenly. She wanted to stick her foot out and trip Becky, who was laughing the hardest. But she just stood there and made her eyes into two skinny slits and watched the group that was completely unaware that she even existed move off across the library.

CHAPTER FOUR

It was early Saturday morning and Figgrotten was already up in her rock room. She wore two sweaters, her brown coat, mittens with liners, and ski socks inside her insulated snow boots. She was warm but this January morning was particularly raw, with a tinfoil-colored sky and air that seemed to ache for snow.

While lying in bed the night before, she'd mapped out her day on the rocks, and now she followed her plan. First she set out the food she'd made for herself: the thermos of hot chocolate, two granola bars, an apple, a honey sandwich, and a bag of potato chips. If she wasn't careful, she'd eat everything before lunch (food tasted a thousand times better when eaten outside), but setting it all out helped her pace herself.

Then she sat on her rock chair and looked down at the house. She could see her mom at the kitchen sink doing last night's dishes. She could see the basement light on in the tiny window under the steps, which meant that was where her dad was. And she could see that Christinia was still asleep, as her room was dark. Christinia used to get up at a normal hour, but now she slept late into the morning, so by the time she finally got up Figgrotten usually had been up for several hours.

Figgrotten took some big breaths of cold air and blew them out. Then she shut her eyes and listened. She could listen deeply if she concentrated enough, listen through layers of sound that would take her far off. Cars out on the main road, wind high up in the white pines, birds deep in the woods. And always, if she waited, she could hear a crow cawing.

That morning she had decided to spend more time watching the crows. She'd brought up a bag of bread crusts that her mom had thrown in the garbage, and when the four crows that always seemed to come around showed up again, she tossed the bread out on the rocks below, then sat and watched. The crows sat for a very long time up in the tree branches, yelling at each other. Then one of them flew down to a lower branch and the other three just about went insane screaming at him. Figgrotten sat with her elbows planted on her knees and her chin in her hands; she was riveted. She watched as the one crow sat for a long, long time, looking all around, clearly making sure the coast was clear. Then, just as she was convinced he would fly down to snatch the bread, the other three crows came down from the trees in total silence and landed next to the bread. The lookout crow was still up on the lower branch, silent and looking around frantically, while his pals sauntered casually below, pecking at the bread. Figgrotten was dying to know how he would get food, and a second later she found out as one of the three crows flew up and landed next to him on the branch and, as if he'd been given permission, the lookout crow flew down and had a little breakfast.

Figgrotten, who had been sitting perfectly still during all this, now opened her notebook and wrote: "Pretty sure crows are not lonely birds. They work as a team and I don't think I've ever seen a crow without a pal."

"Frances!" Her mother was now standing out on the

back porch, calling up to her. "Aren't you freezing up there?"

The crows flew scared into the trees and were looking down at Figgrotten's mom.

"I'm good, Mom. I'm doing a crow study."

"A what?"

"I'm watching those crows." She pointed upward.

Mrs. Pauley stepped forward and craned her neck, looking into the trees, then shrugged and went back inside the house.

Figgrotten leaned back into her notebook and wrote: "Some people hate being alone. Some people like it. I like it a lot. Either that or I'm just sort of used to it."

She paused and looked up into the sky, which felt still and gray and cold. She really didn't feel lonely when she was outside. She felt happy and herself. It was when she was around people that the feeling of being alone was a problem. The feeling of not being quite part of a group was not the best. The solution was simple, though: Be up on the rocks more. Out in the wild.

By eleven it did start to snow, which was terrific. Figgrotten got to see the first flakes, which came down one a minute or so. Then it was two a minute. Then a hundred. Then a thousand. Then beyond that and the air was all snow and she sat getting covered, eating her sandwich, noticing how the birds seemed to rush about trying to get ready for the storm. Noticing how muffled the world became and how, if she listened hard enough, she could hear the snow hitting the ground. It sounded softer than mouse feet on a rug.

At noon Christinia came out onto the back porch and yelled, "You better come inside, you know."

"How come?"

"'Cause there's a storm. Obviously! And when there's a storm you're not supposed to be out in it."

"I'm good, though," Figgrotten called down. "It's nice out." She almost asked if Christinia would come up with her so she could see for herself. But she knew better.

Christinia didn't answer, just turned and went back inside, letting the door slam behind her.

She hadn't always been so miserable.

"Your sister is getting older and that can be hard," her mom said to Figgrotten at one point.

"Why?"

"Because so much changes when you grow up, and sometimes the changes are out of your control and that's kind of scary."

"You mean at school?"

Her mother tended not to interfere between her and Christinia, but now she was trying to help Figgrotten understand. "Yes. But your body changes too—your breasts start to grow and you get a monthly period—and your feelings change too, and it's all a lot. You'll see. It's not easy."

This further confirmed Figgrotten's feeling that she did not want to get older. She enjoyed being the age she was and didn't look forward to changing the way her mother said she would.

But Figgrotten knew these changes were not the only reason that Christinia now hated her. Even though things had been bad between them by the end of summer, Figgrotten was pretty sure the final straw had happened in September when she had gotten called up onto the stage at the school assembly and had been given an award for her summer essay on Margaret Mead. Figgrotten had been called up in front of the entire school, which went from kindergarten all the way through eighth grade, so the place had been packed and there'd been lots of giggling when she'd walked across the stage. She figured this was because she'd been wearing her big rubber rain boots *and* her hat even though it wasn't cold out yet and which she'd put on at the last minute when her name was read aloud. She wasn't quite sure why she'd put her hat on, though later she thought she might have done it out of nervousness. Wearing her hat had a way of sheltering her from the outside world. Anyway, she had put the hat on and walked up and there'd been giggling. The giggling hadn't made her feel bad. It had made her feel she was entertaining everyone a bit. And she had even gone along with it by walking in a slightly funny loping way that made her boots extra loud. But when she'd been standing up getting her award, she had looked into the audience and caught sight of Christinia all slumped down in her seat with her hands over her face. Then, that same afternoon, when she had gotten off the school bus, Christinia had run into the house and up the stairs and slammed her bedroom door. Figgrotten had stood at the bottom of the steps listening to her sobbing.

"What in the world is going on?" her mom had asked, quickly going up the stairs to check on Christinia.

"I don't know," Figgrotten had said, and immediately headed out back to the rocks. But Figgrotten did know. She knew it had just about killed Christinia with embarrassment to see her tromp up there with her hat and rain boots on and get an award for a paper about some weird anthropologist no one had ever even heard of.

And it was after that that Christinia really set about hating her. And the more she hated her, the more set in her ways Figgrotten had become. In other words, there were times she put her hat on just to infuriate Christinia further. Like when she brushed her teeth at night and knew she'd pass Christinia in the hall. Somehow, it was the only way she could get back at Christinia for hating her that much. She was pretty sure this was what a "vicious cycle" was. Another thing Mr. Stanley had taught everyone about. Bad things led to more bad things and round and round everything went.

The snow was now coming down so hard Figgrotten could barely see the house. She'd moved from the rocks to a more sheltered spot under one of the big pine trees and was sitting with her back against it. It gave her almost full protection from the storm and she was able to crack open her encyclopedia without it getting wet. She was pawing through the letter **G**. Sir Galahad; Galveston, Texas; and then she turned the page and saw a picture of Mahatma Gandhi for the first time. A little elfish man wrapped in what looked to be a sheet. Figgrotten leaned forward and read the caption: "Gandhi used peace as his weapon to fight for the rights of the people." She frowned and scrunched her face up. What did that mean? How could you use peace as a weapon? She read on. It said that what he did was simply stand his ground very quietly without yelling and screaming. After she read this, she heard herself say "Oh," and then what felt like a little window in her mind was flung open and a whole new idea came hurtling in.

She called this kind of idea a wrencher, because it had the effect of confusing her set way of thinking.

In her life she'd had these wrenchers only a handful of times. Like when she'd first read about Lucy being one of the oldest people. Or about the universe going on forever, for infinity.

But then she'd also had a wrencher in an unpleasant way, like that time her mom had told her about girls getting their periods. This had been totally startling but it didn't have the same uplifting feeling that the other ideas had had. Though it did shift things inside her. It made her view her sister differently, like she was now someone Figgrotten didn't really know, and it also made her realize that this part of her own life, the life of being a kid, wasn't going to last forever, and this idea brought not an excited feeling but more one of dread tinged with a tugging sadness.

That night at dinner she told her family about Mahatma Gandhi.

"He was sort of cute. I'm thinking I could dress up as him for next Halloween."

Her dad nodded. "Sounds like an easy costume."

Then there was a pause in the conversation before Figgrotten said, "He believed in peace. Like, that is how he actually fought. I didn't know you could fight that way."

"Yes, he did." Her dad nodded again. "It was very effective too."

Her sister looked like she was going to be sick.

Figgrotten took in a breath, then burst out, "I think I believe in peace too." She tried to contain her emotions while she said this, but her voice came out a little too forceful and high and they all glanced at her nervously before her mother said, "That's so nice, Frances." Then changed the subject and said, "I think this rice needs some salt."

Later, while her family was watching TV, Figgrotten sat on the floor of her room with her window open. She could tell it was still snowing. Not only could she still hear the softness of it coming down, but little drifts piled up on her windowsill and blew onto the floor. She was deeply bundled with her coat and hat and gloves on, and her breath was coming out in little white puffs. She was organizing her finds. She had quite a collection. Birds' nests (one of which she had found on the ground during a field trip to the Cream River Farm and which was made almost entirely of horse hair), crazy leaves that were the size of dinner plates, hickory nuts that had absolutely perfect holes gnawed in them, rocks with mica shining inside them. She had laid these out in a trail that went all the way around the edge of the room, stopping only for the doorway.

Figgrotten remembered the conversation that she had with her mom a couple of months before, when her mom gave up coming into her room. Figgrotten was now pretty sure she was starting to understand what her mom had been talking about. Everything in her room was super-duper dusty and there were big hairy dust bunnies under her bed. But the idea of picking up all her things, which she had organized in a way that was important to her, was sort of out of the question at the moment. She was on her hands and knees now, looking over each one. The clay marble that she'd found in the stream across the road from her house that she had convinced herself could have only been made by a Native American. The absolutely perfect half of a blue robin's egg.

Around nine o'clock Figgrotten's mom called up that it was bedtime, so Figgrotten went into the bathroom to brush her teeth and get ready for bed. She had another day planned up on the rocks in the snow, and she did want to get an early start. She stood in the bathroom brushing her teeth and staring into the mirror. Her hat covered a lot of her face, so she studied her eyes and nose mostly. It was just her face. She was so used to it she usually didn't give it a second thought. The only thing about it at the moment that she wanted to change was she sort of wished she could have a pair of round glasses like Gandhi had.

Heading back to her bedroom, she stopped at the top of the stairs and heard the TV still going down in the living room. They were watching some movie that sounded kind of scary. Figgrotten tiptoed back down the hall and stopped in front of Christinia's door. It was open and she looked into her sister's room, which was spotless and neat. Her eyes scanned the posters of horses and some singer who Christinia was in love with, her schoolbooks perfectly piled on her desk, her guitar leaning against the wall. But Figgrotten froze when she saw her sister's journal lying wide open on her bed. She felt her heart suddenly speed up. She leaned back to hear the TV still going, then she crept very quietly into Christinia's room and looked down at the page with her sister's tiny and perfect handwriting. She stood there just for a second. Then she turned and tiptoed silently back out into the hall. The TV was still on.

When she got back into her room, she let out a big breath and sat down on the side of her bed. She hadn't exactly read the journal. She'd simply looked at the page and had picked out a few words. *Becky. Mean. Hate.* Those were three of them. This confirmed something that she had sensed. But it was the other two words that had made her breath catch and now were swirling around in her head. One was *like* and the other was *Ben. Ben. Ben. Ben.* There was a lot about a Ben in there. And for the second time that day, an all-new thought came hurtling into her mind and rearranged all her old thoughts. It was another thought-wrencher.

Christinia liked a boy.

CHAPTER FIVE

The only Ben she knew of was Ben Ekhart, one of the boys who made burping noises and threw things at the backs of the other kids' heads. Could it possibly be this Ben her sister had written about?

On Monday morning, Figgrotten stood on the side of the road and made drawings in the snow with her feet. Only when the bus pulled up did Christinia charge out of the house and run across the yard. She pushed Figgrotten aside and climbed on in front of her, marching to the back and plopping down hard in her seat. Then she went into her slumped position, staring out the window.

The snow had been cleared off the roads and was piled up high on the sides. The world looked stunned and brilliant under the clean layer. Little bones of snow lay on top of each branch, and when they drove past the Tierneys' dairy farm, the big cornfields were pristine oceans of whiteness. Figgrotten couldn't imagine living in a place where there weren't seasons like there were in Preston. Seasons, she thought happily, changed the world so dramatically. Life would get so dull without tangly hot green summers, then cold snowy winters.

She glanced up and looked at Alvin in his rearview mirror. She had a perfect view of his face under his black Greek fisherman's hat, and she stared at it lovingly for a minute before he glanced up and caught her eye.

"What's going through that mind of yours, young lady?" Alvin said.

Figgrotten slid forward on her seat and raised her voice. "Alvin, do you like to be alone or do you like to be around people?"

"Both. Everyone needs both. Solitude and friendship."

Figgrotten sat back in her seat and looked out the window. She kind of wished he'd just said "Alone."

Then she leaned forward again and said, "Alvin, have you ever heard of Mahatma Gandhi?"

"Yes, oh, certainly."

"I think you look like him a little."

"I'll take that as a compliment."

Figgrotten pushed herself back into the seat and clamped down on her lips. She knew she could potentially drive Alvin insane with all her thoughts and questions, so she always held herself back a little with him. But after another minute she slid forward again and said, "I really like him. He wasn't a fighter."

Alvin nodded and smiled. "Oh, Miss Pauley, there you are wrong, he was indeed a fighter. But he fought very gently and without violence of any kind. And that always is more powerful than using weapons."

Figgrotten nodded. Alvin knew everything there was to know.

He slowed the bus, as there was James Barren, standing behind a huge snowbank. Figgrotten craned her neck to see him through the windshield. His mom wasn't with him this time. Figgrotten was sure glad she'd never had to start at a new school. People wouldn't know what to make of her, and when kids were faced with something different, she knew, sometimes they lashed out in response.

Alvin opened the door and James struggled through the knee-deep snow in his sneakers.

"Good morning," Alvin said as he climbed on. James said a very quiet hello, then looked down the aisle. He stood still for a second, then threw his knapsack into the seat behind Figgrotten's and sat down. She didn't turn to look at him as the bus roared forward, but if she looked out the window at things and sort of turned her head to follow them, she could see James out of the corner of her eye. He was slouched down in his seat reading a book, his head down and his hair hanging around his face. She wanted to know what he was reading, but there was no way she was talking to him or turning around to look.

Of course, she wished he hadn't sat there, because now she found herself not wanting to talk to Alvin about Gandhi. So she slid back in her seat and watched the snowy town go by.

When they pulled into the school, Figgrotten did her usual scan of the teachers' lot for Mr. Stanley's car, and she gave a tiny sigh of relief at the sight of the minuscule thing, pulled at an angle at the farthest corner. It was the smallest car Figgrotten had ever seen. In fact, when she'd first laid eyes on the vehicle a year back, she couldn't quite figure out if it was even a whole car. It seemed to be half of one.

"It uses only one gallon of gas for every sixty miles of driving," Mr. Stanley had told the class when it had come up in conversation. Though, clearly, no one seemed to care about such things. Figgrotten was far more concerned about how tiny the car was. It could barely fit one other passenger, let alone a dog and a kid. What it was, Figgrotten surmised, was a car for one person with no plans to be more than one person. She wasn't sure how she felt about this, but it made her think Mr. Stanley was different. And she realized this being different was one of the things she liked about him.

School felt a bit crazy for the first hour that day. All because of the snow and the things kids came to school wearing. The voluminous snowsuits seemed to take up the entire hallway. Snow boots had been flung left and right. No one cared a hoot about classwork; the whole day was focused on heading out the door for recess. Figgrotten was no exception. She normally found the classroom overheated and stuffy, but today it felt twice so. As Mr. Stanley began the morning, talking about the date of the science fair and how no one was allowed to chew gum in the classroom, Figgrotten stared out the window at the blindingly white snow. It shone in the sun, and each bird that flew across it was a splash of color and movement. She longed to dive into its coldness.

Then Mr. Stanley clapped his hands together, which made Figgrotten sit up. "Today we're going to talk about one big word," he said, and walked up to the chalkboard and wrote CIVILIZATION in huge letters across it. Then he stood back and put his hands on his hips and looked around the classroom.

"Okay, folks, I would bet we all sort of think we know what this word means. But go ahead, give it a crack. Anyone?"

Figgrotten glanced around the room and saw, as always, a lot of blank faces. But then a hand went up in the front.

"Yes, James?"

"It means when a group of people act civilized or, like, not completely . . . I don't know, crazy?" James said.

Figgrotten suddenly felt a jolt of something unpleasant go through her.

"Aha! Yes. But what does being civilized mean?"

Her hand went up. But before Mr. Stanley could call on her, James said, "It means people not fighting with each other?" And Mr. Stanley nodded and turned and wrote CIVILIZED = NOT FIGHTING on the chalkboard while Figgrotten's hand sank down.

"Can anyone add to this?" Mr. Stanley asked.

James's hand went back up, and Figgrotten put her hand up again, but then so did Marshall Wolff. He never put his hand up, so of course Mr. Stanley called on him.

"Does it have to do with, like, not being cavemen?"

"Oh, wonderful, that's right, Marshall," Mr. Stanley said, and went back to the board and wrote, BEING A CIVILIAN = NOT BEING A CAVEMAN. Then he said, "However, what part about being civilized is not like being a caveman?"

Figgrotten raised her hand and so did a few other kids, but James just blurted out, "Following rules or laws."

Figgrotten felt herself slide down in her seat and at the same time felt her face scrunch up like she smelled something bad. James had answered too many questions. She glanced around and, sure enough, her classmates also were slumping now.

"That's right, James. Very good. A civilization is when a society is advanced in a way where people can live together under certain rules. Were the Native Americans a civilization?"

Clearly Mr. Stanley was so excited by how smart James was that he didn't notice he wasn't always following the rule about raising your hand to speak.

So now Figgrotten didn't even put up her hand.

"Definitely," James said, just blurting out again.

Mr. Stanley then walked back to Figgrotten's desk. "Did you have something you'd like to add, Frances?"

Figgrotten sat up now and shrugged a little. She wanted to say something about Gandhi suddenly. She was pretty sure he might be a good example of someone who acted in a civilized way. "Well, I guess, being civilized is like waiting your turn to be called on. Stuff like that. Following rules."

Mr. Stanley smiled at her. "Yes," he said. "Those are examples." She wasn't quite sure if he got her hint about James or not.

When recess finally did come, Figgrotten had to fight her way through the mad chaos to get to her locker and get her snow pants and boots on. There was barely anything civilized about any of it. By the time she got outside, much of the perfect snow had been trampled on, but she found a nice clean patch out by the fence, away from the mounds of screaming kids, and she lay down and made a snow angel and stared up at the sky.

She lay there until she could feel the cold coming through her clothes, which took away the hot closed-in feel of the classroom and gave her a tiny bit of a wonderful feeling. Freedom. She closed her eyes and listened as kids raced by and screamed and laughed. She was happy enough being by herself, but she felt aware of it now more than she used to. She'd think, *I'm alone, which is fine.* Whereas before, she was just alone and didn't think about it.

She closed her eyes and lay still, feeling the winter sun on her face. She wished the eighth graders had recess at the same time as her, because then maybe she could quietly observe and figure out what was going on with her sister. She knew of only one other Ben in the school, and he was in fourth grade and was about three feet tall. So he couldn't be the Ben Christinia liked. Which left only the bad one from the bus. Ben Ekhart.

Alvin, as always, was sitting behind the wheel reading his book when Figgrotten climbed back onto the bus that afternoon. He read with the page up close to his eyes, but he still greeted each person who came onto the bus. "Miss Pauley," he said as Figgrotten climbed on. She sat in her seat, but then stood halfway up and looked over Alvin's shoulder and read the title of the book, *Black Elk Speaks,* out loud.

Alvin nodded. "I read it a long time ago and it never left me. So here I am, reading it again."

"Is that him? That's Black Elk?" Figgrotten pointed at the picture of the Native American on the cover. He was wearing a fur hat and earrings and a really big necklace.

"Indeed it is," Alvin said, nodding. "I think everyone should read it at some point in their lives. It's not easy, though. It's quite a sad book."

"Oh. Okay." Figgrotten sat back in her seat. She'd try to remember the title and write it in her journal later, though she wasn't crazy about the idea of reading something that was sad.

Alvin nodded again slowly. Then he sighed and put the book down in his lap. "Now, Miss Pauley, on another subject, after talking with you this morning about Gandhi, I went to the library and wrote down a couple of famous things that Gandhi said that I thought you might like to have on hand." He closed the book and then reopened it to the first page and pulled out a little piece of paper with his raggedy handwriting on it, and when he handed it back to her she noticed the paper was shaking. It was the first time she'd ever noticed

Alvin's hand shaking like that. She took the paper and looked down and read under her breath.

> "You must not lose faith in humanity. Humanity is an ocean; if a few drops of the ocean are dirty, the ocean does not become dirty.
>
> "An eye for an eye only ends up making the whole world blind."

"Now, those are just a couple of notions for you to ponder when you're up in your rock world."

Figgrotten sat looking down at the paper. The handwriting was so jaggedy that it suddenly made her feel sad. It was *too* jaggedy. "Thanks, I'll try to figure out what they mean."

"Yes, you do that." Alvin leaned forward and started the bus. "Ah, the world is a wild and exciting place, but sometimes, so it doesn't get too wild and exciting, people need to be reminded how to behave. Gandhi was quite good at that."

As the bus pulled out onto the road, Figgrotten very much wanted to lean forward and tell Alvin about Mr. Stanley's discussion about the word *civilization,* but once again James had sat down behind her and she didn't want him interjecting.

But Alvin started talking anyway, so all she had to do was scooch forward in her seat and listen.

"Now, Miss Pauley, I read in the science section of the paper today that they may have discovered a whole other planet out there in our solar system. And when I read this, I just about lifted off my chair in the library. I mean, here we all are toodling along thinking we've figured it all out, and *poof!* . . . wrong . . . there's a discovery like this."

Alvin shook his head and let out his high cackling laugh. This laugh was music to Figgrotten's ears, as it had never stopped being startling and funny.

"I always forget about stuff that's not on Earth," Figgrotten said to Alvin. "And then I look up at the sky and I—"

"Wait, let me tell you—your mind can't fathom it!" Alvin said, lifting his two skinny hands off the steering wheel for a fraction of a second, then plunking them back down again. Then he let out another crazy laugh and Figgrotten sat back in her seat smiling.

"Yes, exactly," she said, and looked out the window.

Just then she heard something in the back of the bus that made her turn around in her seat just in time to see Becky Moss get out of her seat and walk slowly, comically swinging her hips, to the back seat, where she plopped down right next to Ben Ekhart. The look on Becky's face was the kind of look you'd get if you'd just won the prize for most popular kid on the planet. Or had managed to get the biggest slice of cake at a party. She looked that pleased with herself. Everyone was clapping and hooting and laughing. Figgrotten turned slowly back around in her seat, letting her eyes slide over the other kids until she caught sight of Christinia, who had now slipped so low in her seat it was hard to see her at first. But once Figgrotten caught sight of her, she recognized immediately the look on her sister's face. Christinia was holding back from crying. Figgrotten froze, staring, which was the worst thing she could have done, because Christinia glanced up suddenly and their eyes met.

Oh boy, Figgrotten thought as she spun around, *now I'm in for it.*

CHAPTER SIX

Figgrotten was now officially doing an experiment with crows. She decided that each day when she went up to her rocks to do homework, she'd bring a little snack for them, which she'd put in the same place at the same time each day. And each time she'd do it, she'd whistle, and eventually, if her experiment worked, the crows would hear the whistle and come when she called. She was a terrific whistler. Her dad had taught her how to whistle for a taxi if she ever went to New York City. He used to live there and told her how you stand on the corner, stick two fingers of one hand in your mouth, and blow while waving the other hand up in the air. She'd loved watching him do this so much that she spent an entire week learning to whistle, and now she was a pro.

So today, when she got up on her rocks, she scattered a few pieces of bread out below her on a lower rock ledge, looked up into the trees for the crows, saw hide nor hair of them, and stuck her fingers in her mouth and let loose a loud whistle. Then she sat down and got to work.

It was kind of difficult doing homework up on the rocks with all the snow. It was hard not to get her books and papers wet, and writing with her gloves on was awkward. But she cleared away as much snow as possible and sat down to get to work on her dreaded math.

Once she had asked Mr. Stanley why on earth anyone had to do math beyond adding and subtracting and multiplying. And Mr. Stanley had said it was simple, that human beings had brains and not learning math was a waste of a brain. "Your brain needs exercise just like your body does. If you don't use it, it stops working. If you use it, it works better." Now here again was an example of why Mr. Stanley was so fantastic.

Figgrotten hated the idea of a brain going to waste. Thinking was such a terrific thing. Though sometimes, when she was thinking about thinking, she would start to wonder what exactly thoughts were. They sure came into her head a lot. Occasionally she would close her eyes and attempt to stop thinking, which was difficult. But this was how she had become such a good listener. The minute she stopped her thinking, she could hear everything. And this made her imagine what it must have been like being a tiny baby. Babies, she figured, didn't think much, because they didn't know any words. She imagined herself as a tiny baby just hearing, seeing, smelling, and feeling but not really thinking. Thinking probably began to happen when she put words to things. *Mommy. Daddy. Christinia. Bird. Tree.* This was the kind of thing she needed to talk to Alvin about at some point. He'd have something interesting to say about this.

That afternoon, when she was almost done with her math, one of the crows flew into a nearby tree. Figgrotten put down her pencil and sat very still. She watched the crow looking down at the bread. He sat tilting his head from one direction to the other. Listening, she figured, and looking. And then he let out four loud, evenly spaced caws: "Caw! Caw! Caw! Caw!" Then he waited and Figgrotten waited and sure enough the other crows soon arrived, one after the other landing quietly in nearby trees. And now all four crows sat looking at the bread until one, then two, then three flew down and had an afternoon snack while the fourth sat looking around frantically.

That evening before bed, in her nice cold room, Figgrotten wrote in her journal.

> Whistled for crows when putting bread out for them. They came but not from the whistle. From the bread smell most likely. But I think they are way smarter than any one of us walking around down here on the ground knows. I think they have things figured out about life.
>
> I think Christinia wants a boyfriend, which is gross. I don't like boys, I have decided. Especially James Barren, who thinks he's so smart. He's so annoying.

When she was done writing, she went to the window and looked outside. There was an almost-full moon in the sky, and it lit up the woods behind the house with its bluish light. Figgrotten opened her window as far as it would go and leaned her body out into the cold air, and listened very hard. She wasn't hoping to hear anything. In fact, it was the opposite. She was listening to the amazing deep quiet that the night often held.

But her listening session didn't last long. Someone knocked on her door and she turned just as Christinia stepped inside. She shut the door quietly, then turned to Figgrotten and put her hands on her hips.

"What?" Figgrotten's heart started thumping now.

"You need to mind your own business." Christinia was talking in a low voice but her tone was forceful and bitter. "You're constantly spying on me. And I'm going to kill you if you keep doing it."

Figgrotten felt her face get red with anger. "What are you talking about? Why would I want to spy on you and your stupid boring life? And you're going to kill me? That means you're going to murder me?" She surprised herself that it had come out of her mouth in such a super-snotty know-it-all way. She had never talked to anyone like this before. In fact, she sounded like Christinia did most of the time, and it amazed her that she was capable of pulling off the same thing herself.

Christinia looked startled at first; then she took another step into Figgrotten's room and narrowed her eyes and lowered her voice even more. "You know what you are? You are a freak. A little ugly freak and you're ruining my life. You want to know what I did, I told my friends that we aren't even related. I told them you were adopted. That's how much I hate having you as a sister." She brought her hand, which had been behind her back, out in front of her and Figgrotten saw she was holding the card with her name on it that had been tacked to her door. Christinia crumpled it in her hand and threw it as hard as she could across the room. Then she turned and left, slamming the door so hard that two branches that were propped up against the wall came clattering down.

Figgrotten stood still for a second, unable to breathe; then she gasped and ran to her bed and threw herself across it, planting her face into her pillow and letting out a muffled scream of rage. Then uncontrollable sobs took hold of her entire body, and she lay there convulsing from them. Why did she have such a horrible, evil person as a sister? She hated Christinia more than anyone else on earth. Hated her. Hate, hate, hated her! That she'd called her an ugly freak was terrible, but that she'd lied to her friends and told them she was adopted—this seared her, and burned her like a hot pan. All the unfriendliness Christinia had doled out to her up to this point paled in comparison to those words. They were mean-spirited lies, but worse than anything else, they were unbearably embarrassing. It humiliated Figgrotten to think she'd been talked about in this way among a group of eighth-grade girls. She screamed again into her pillow when she thought of it. She wanted to go into Christinia's room and make her take it back. Take back what she'd told those girls. Take it back. But Figgrotten didn't. She just stayed lying face-down on her bed, sobbing and sobbing.

Finally, when she was able to control herself, she rolled over and tried to breathe, but her breath was all stuttery and tears kept rolling down the sides of her face and into her ears.

She looked around her room. There were her trees and her Lucy poster and her pictures of the life cycle of the duck-billed platypus. There was also the picture of Margaret Mead that she'd printed out in the library at school last year. It was of the anthropologist standing among a tribe of almost-naked people. She couldn't have looked more different from all those people. Her heavy skirt and buttoned-up jacket, her glasses, the sturdy lace-up shoes. Not to mention her walking stick. But it was the expression on her face that Figgrotten stared at. She didn't exactly look happy. Figgrotten thought for a minute and it came to her: Mead looked determined. *I am going to be determined,* Figgrotten thought. *I'm determined to never speak to Christinia ever again.* It was the only way she began to feel a little better, making this plan to never talk to her sister ever again. *It's over,* she thought.

Figgrotten's eyes now fell to the floor where the crumpled card with her name on it lay. She stood and picked it up and smoothed it open and stared down at her handwriting. She'd been younger when she'd named herself this, and her handwriting was that of a first grader, not a fifth grader. Suddenly her old writing made her horribly sad. She slipped the wrinkled card into her journal and slid the little book under her pillow, and then she lay down on her side with her knees tucked up near her chest and her hands clasped together under her chin. It was what people who prayed did, she thought. She was not exactly a prayer, but she was a hoper. And now she fell asleep hoping that she could stick to her plan and never have anything to do with her horrible sister ever, ever again.

CHAPTER SEVEN

The next morning Figgrotten stood waiting for the bus. She had her hat pulled farther down on her head than usual in an attempt to cover her eyes, which were still swollen from crying the night before. It was a sharp, cold morning, and to keep from freezing, she jogged in place a bit, watching the little puffs of white breath go out into the air in front of her. Not once had she ever missed the bus the way Christinia sometimes did. In fact, she went out ten minutes early each morning so she could breathe in some nice outdoor air and check out the birds. She knew now that certain birds were a sign of certain seasons. Some were passing through on their way north or south. Some only came and stayed in the summer. Some were there year-round, like the crows.

Today she had her eyes out for her crows. Somehow, setting her mind on doing this helped her get out of bed and kept her from going over the awful interaction with Christinia. So far there'd been no sign of the crows, though. She wondered where they were when they weren't around. How far did they fly off? Mainly she wanted to know if they had certain patterns she could depend on. She stood looking up into the pine trees behind her house, and while she stood there, she heard the school bus approaching.

When the bus pulled up and the door opened, there was Alvin with his hat on, smiling at her. "Good morning, Miss Pauley. Any birds this morning?"

Figgrotten smiled, shrugged, and climbed up the steps, but something sad felt stuck in her throat and she couldn't quite talk.

"Where's that sister of yours?" Alvin was craning his neck looking toward the house.

"I think she's sick today," Figgrotten heard herself say, which was pretty much a lie. The words just came right out of her mouth. But as Alvin began to pull away, Figgrotten caught sight of the front door opening, and before the bus lumbered around the corner, she saw her sister run onto the front lawn frantically waving. Someone else must have seen this too, because they yelled from the back and Alvin slammed on the brakes and opened the door.

"Oh, no, not sick. Just late!" he laughed.

When Christinia climbed on, out of breath, Figgrotten slid down low in her seat and kept her head turned toward the window. She refused to even look at her sister. Christinia had told those girls she was adopted? Figgrotten felt a lump starting in her throat, and her eyes began to burn as if she was about to cry. So she sat up and took a deep breath and tried to think of Clark, purring and lying upside down in her arms.

When she looked up a minute later, there was Alvin looking hard at her in the rearview mirror, as if he was trying to make out something in the distance.

"Now, Miss Pauley, did I ever tell you that I went to a great big school in New York City when I was a boy? Oh, it was a terrific school, as many schools were back then. I had a few teachers who made all the difference in my life. One of them was a French teacher who wore very elegant suits every day. It turned out his family owned the foremost suit-making business in Vienna, and so there he was, wearing these suits every day.

Impeccable and elegant. So out of place in that setting. Teaching all these little kids French. I remember knowing that despite how rich he was, he wanted to be a teacher, and this made quite an impact on how I felt about him."

Figgrotten nodded and sat listening to Alvin. She loved it when he talked about his life. She imagined him as a little skinny kid with his Greek fisherman's cap on.

"Do you still know how to speak French?" she now asked him.

"Mais oui," he laughed. "*Mais oui,* but yes! For your information."

"Mais oui," Figgrotten echoed. She sat back in her seat and looked out the window and tried not to think about Christinia.

A few minutes later, when James climbed on and sat down behind Figgrotten again, she felt herself stiffen. If he had spoken to her, she was pretty sure she might have told him to bug off. Or to get a life. Or, worse than anything, she might have said nothing, giving him an icy stare that would have said it all. Just like Christinia had taught her. A glare that could make everything inside a person droop and feel dreadful. She disliked James, though she wasn't sure why, other than he clearly knew he was smart but didn't know how to use his smartness in a way that didn't make other people feel bad.

Figgrotten was quieter than usual in class, and twice when Mr. Stanley called on her she had to be reminded what he was talking about. She kept staring out the window, going over her fight with Christinia. She did notice, however, that James once again had his hand up a lot but was also blurting out the correct answers to lots of the math problems. Figgrotten could feel how impressed Mr. Stanley was with each of his answers, the way he always had been with her, and this only made her sink down farther in her chair.

During recess that day, Figgrotten didn't go out onto the playground. Instead she sat alone at a picnic table against the building and watched the other kids playing. The only other girl who was alone was mousy old Fiona Peterson. Figgrotten watched her as she walked along the perimeter of the playground dragging a long stick and singing to herself. If a gust of wind blew through the place, she was pretty sure Fiona would just go hurtling off into the air. She was that wispy and boring. Figgrotten scrunched up her nose and looked around. Only then did she realize that James wasn't out on the playground either. He was sitting cross-legged not far from her, with his back up against the building, but he wasn't looking too lonely. He was slumped over a big book that sat open in his lap, fully engrossed, clearly not giving a hoot about any kid out on that playground. Once again Figgrotten felt a stab of something unpleasant go through her. Something a little mean. It bothered her to see him sitting like that outdoors. She was alone too, but she wasn't alone like him. If someone had come and talked to her, she would have talked back to them. But no one would go up to James when he was reading a book. It was stupid. *He* was stupid.

"Mr. Stanley," Figgrotten said, suddenly standing up. "Can I go to the bathroom?"

"Yes, you *may*." Mr. Stanley, who was standing by the door, gave her the correction gently and handed her the little wooden block that said GIRLS' ROOM on it.

"Frances," he said, "just checking in with you—is everything all right today? You seem a bit distracted."

Figgrotten nodded.

"Well, okay. If there is something bothering you, you can let me know. You know that, right?"

"Okay," she said softly, and turned and went down the hall.

She couldn't very well tell Mr. Stanley what was bothering her. She couldn't tell him that her sister was evil and horrible and mean. Or that James was stupid for thinking he was so smart. Or that she wanted to be home, up on her rocks, not here at school. These weren't things you talked about with your teacher.

Figgrotten didn't actually need to use the bathroom, so once she was in it, she killed time by looking at herself in the mirror, which, to be honest, was something she rarely did. Not that she had an aversion to what she saw, more that she'd already seen plenty of herself, so what more was there to see?

Today her hair was in a particularly interesting shape, which was most likely due to her having slept under her blankets last night and then putting her hat on immediately when she woke up. Her hair was half flattened against her head and half sticking out in a triangular shape at the bottom. Figgrotten eyed it but didn't so much as reach up to try to rearrange it. She didn't quite understand why it mattered what she looked like, although she knew she was somewhat alone in this particular view. Besides, there were okay things about the way she looked. She had large brown eyes and nice eyelashes, and when she smiled, she had two dimples like little parentheses around her mouth. She could be worse. She could have a lopsided face with one eye on her forehead and another down on her chin. Her mother often told her she was a "hidden beauty," which Figgrotten did not like. She was certain it was the kind of thing you said to someone who wasn't, in fact, beautiful.

Suddenly, while she was standing looking into the mirror, the bathroom door burst open and two seventh-grade girls came in, chatting loudly. When they saw her, they both stopped; then one of them, Figgrotten wasn't sure which because she'd turned away, made a loud gagging sound like she was about to throw up, after which they melted into uncontrollable laughter.

"Oh, *gross*!" the other one said.

Figgrotten had a horrible dipping feeling down through her belly. Her mouth fell open to say something, but this time words just clumped in her throat and she felt her eyes start to burn once again, like she was about to cry. Then she did what she knew she shouldn't do, but somehow, in a moment of terrible weakness, she just turned and fled. Out of the bathroom and down the hall she ran, and then, without thinking what she was doing, she turned in to the nurse's office. The school nurse, Mrs. Bellamy, was a plump woman with a sweet, soft voice. She was so wonderfully kind that all the kids, including Figgrotten, adored her.

"Frances," she said when Figgrotten stepped into her little office, "I rarely get the pleasure of seeing you in here. Now, do tell me what's the matter, sweetheart."

Figgrotten opened her mouth but once again found that her words had slipped away, and for the third time in twenty-four hours her eyes filled with tears.

Mrs. Bellamy tilted her head to one side and almost seemed about to cry herself.

"Oh, dear girl," she said softly. "If you'd like to tell me what's bothering you, I might be able to help."

Figgrotten shook her head. She couldn't.

"Would you like me to call your mom?"

Figgrotten nodded and sat down and Mrs. Bellamy put her big warm hand on Figgrotten's forehead and then shook her head. "You're cool as a cucumber." She took hold of one of Figgrotten's hands while she dialed the phone.

"Mrs. Pauley, good afternoon, it's Darlene. Frances is here and I think she'd like you to come pick her up." There was a pause; then she said, "No, I don't think so, but I think she isn't feeling perfect." Another pause. "Yes, yes . . . see you in a few minutes. No need to rush." Then she put the phone down and sat for a minute still holding Figgrotten's hand. Figgrotten was trying to keep herself together, but she was unable to stop the tears from sliding down her face, and her breath was all hiccuppy. She was so grateful to Mrs. Bellamy for calling her mom so quickly without too many questions.

"Frances, I just hope and pray someone was not unkind to you." Mrs. Bellamy shook her head and sighed. "Because I rarely see tears like this that aren't from some kind of hurt in here." She pointed at her heart, then sighed and stood up. She walked to the water cooler and got Figgrotten a little paper cup of ice-cold water, which Figgrotten drank and which, for some reason, made her feel slightly better.

It took only a few minutes for her mom to get to the school. She came into the nurse's office with an alarmed look on her face and held Figgrotten's hand as they walked out of the building.

The car felt so quiet. So warm. Figgrotten sank down in the seat and looked out the window.

"Oh, Frances," her mom sighed. "Please tell me what happened."

But Figgrotten shook her head. She couldn't talk.

"Honey, it's very important not to bottle up your feelings. It really can make things so much worse. So I hope we can talk about all this later when you feel up to it."

For whatever reason, these words made the tears

now pour from Figgrotten's eyes, and her mom reached across and took her hand and a few minutes later they were home.

As always, being up on the rocks, in the cold air, would make her feel better, she thought as she climbed the zigzag path. That and being by herself. It didn't matter at that moment that Alvin said everyone needed people. Figgrotten knew for her it wasn't true. Not now, anyway. Now she needed to be alone. Once she got up there, she closed her eyes for a second. It was so quiet, just a little breeze hushing through the pines. Nothing could have felt more comforting after such a terrible, dreadful twenty-four hours.

She put some bread crusts down for the crows and whistled, though her whistle was weak compared to the day before. Then she sat down and opened her math book, but she couldn't focus on her work. She wasn't sure what was more upsetting, Christinia telling her eighth-grade friends she was adopted or the stupid seventh-grade girls in the bathroom. But suddenly it felt like everyone thought she was weird. Not just her horrible sister. And somehow this made just being herself a whole new thing. A thing that made her stomach twist into a knot. Both incidents kept replaying in her mind. Over and over again.

Later the crows arrived, dropping one by one off

the tree to eat the bread. Again Figgrotten put down her pencil and leaned her chin on her hand and watched them intently. So far she wasn't sure her experiment was working. She had the feeling they were showing up only when they saw the bread. She wasn't sure her whistle was making an impact. Their blackness shone against the white snow. She'd never thought this before, but now she saw that not only were they intelligent, they were truly magnificent creatures. They were so beautiful and brilliant that somehow just seeing them lifted something up inside of her. She sat watching the way they worked together, three of them landing and picking at the bread, one of them staying up in the tree listening and standing guard. Then that one flying down and another one flying up and taking over the lookout job. After a bit, she sighed and went back to her math, focusing hard on just the problems at hand, each with one answer, nice and neat, without any feelings involved. It made her realize this was one thing math was good for.

CHAPTER EIGHT

The crows started waking her up every morning that week. They would sit up in the pine trees behind her house and make a big old racket, cawing back and forth to each other. She'd climb out of bed and stick her head out the window and see them up in the swaying branches of the pine trees, bobbing in the cold wind. She was pretty sure they had never done this before, and she had to wonder if this new habit of theirs had to do with her feeding them.

The bottom line was that animals were mysterious. You could never read their minds. She sure wished you could, though. She wished she knew what Clark was thinking. Like when he would sit on the back porch and just stare out in front of him. Kind of like he was in a trance. She'd wonder, *What the devil is he thinking?*

Sometimes she wondered what went through certain people's brains as well. Fiona Peterson was one of these people who, for some reason, Figgrotten would wonder about. She was so quiet and so mousy, but there was something about her that was different too. Figgrotten knew Fiona was smart, because she always had the right answers when Mr. Stanley called on her, and finished all her tests before most kids. But Figgrotten hadn't a clue what went on inside her.

Then there was James. She definitely wondered what he was thinking when he blurted out answers without being called on, and when he sat with his book out on the playground. Did he ever think about anyone but himself? It didn't seem that way. But who knew?

Sometimes she even wondered what went through Alvin's mind. Especially that morning, as he seemed distracted, his mind off in the distance. It was as if he was trying to figure out a problem inside his head and couldn't get it. She'd been watching him in the bus's rearview mirror at moments when he seemed lost in thought.

"There was a full moon last night, Alvin," she told

him at one point, knowing this usually could get him going on some subject.

But he just nodded and said, "Oh, is that so?" And then she saw him grimace as if someone had just pinched him.

A few minutes later there was a commotion in the back of the bus and two of the big kids started wrestling. They even fell off their seats for a second and rolled around in the aisle. Everyone was screaming and clapping and laughing. But the weirdest thing was, Alvin didn't seem to notice.

Figgrotten sat back and stared out the window and felt once again the knot in her stomach tightening. On top of everything else, she was worried that Alvin wasn't acting like himself.

Because of the extra-early cawing alarm clock, Figgrotten was ready for school early each day that week, and she'd sit in the kitchen with her mom, eating toast and watching the clock. Upstairs she'd hear Christinia stomping and slamming the door, the shower going, the hair dryer howling. Each time a door slammed, she'd roll her eyes and she and her mom would exchange a quick look.

"You'll see," her mom would then say. "It will happen to you."

But Figgrotten was determined to not let *it* happen to her. She doubted Margaret Mead had ever acted like this.

She thought a lot about Mead lately. She kept thinking about how she might have handled certain things. The girls in the bathroom, for instance. What would old Margaret have done? Figgrotten was pretty sure she knew. Mead would have been able to look at the whole incident as an observer. She probably wouldn't have taken it personally and would have just questioned what made seventh-grade girls act like that. Figgrotten wished she could do that. But it wasn't easy. Going over the episode still made her stomach tighten into a hard knot.

But without her wanting it to, something *had* started to shift inside her. Now at night when she lay in her dark cold room, she could sense a change. It had started with Christinia saying that she was a freak, followed by the incident with the stupid girls in the bathroom. Now when she pulled her big hat on to keep her ears warm, the word would come into her head. *Freak*. She kept imagining how she'd been sailing along before that word was used on her. Just breezing along, in fact. But suddenly there was a feeling that all that nice breeze had stopped. And her sails had drooped. And she was stalled. And if she could come up with a noise inside herself, it was this: *blah.* Just that. Just *blah.*

Luckily, that Friday Mr. Stanley made his whipped-cream cupcakes for Martin Luther King's birthday and had everyone sit around in a big circle listening to King's "I Have a Dream" speech while he served them on his little blue glass plates. They were chocolate with a whipped-cream filling, and they were the greatest thing Figgrotten had ever eaten. Mr. Stanley made them four times a year. Once on the first day of school. Once on the day before Thanksgiving. Once on Martin Luther King's birthday, and finally in June, on the last day of school.

Figgrotten had heard Dr. King's speech a bunch of times now, and every time, it gave her goose bumps up and down her arms. But this year felt different. This time the speech filled her with a strong urge to actually do something to make sure people were never treated unfairly. And it made her angry to know that Martin Luther King had died just because he stood up for what was right. Same with Gandhi. It showed that their peacefulness scared people almost as much as if they'd been waving a gun around. Suddenly, while she listened to Dr. King's voice, she had an awful feeling that she was about to start crying. The speech made her sad every time she heard it. She glanced around the circle and saw that none of the other kids looked upset; they were eating their cupcakes and horsing around. The only other person who looked as sad as she felt was James. He sat listening, his head tilted a little to one side, and his cupcake was uneaten on his plate.

She could tell James got the speech the way she did, and Figgrotten once again felt a jab of something mean and she narrowed her eyes at him, though he was too caught up in the words of Martin Luther King to notice.

As she rode home on the bus that same day, there was yet another huge riotous whooping and hollering from the back seats. But once again Alvin didn't do anything. He wasn't looking up into the mirror as usual. Figgrotten had a feeling this time that she really should not turn around again. *Don't do it,* she told herself. *Do not turn.* But the whistling and the laughter coming from back there was a new level of loudness and wildness. So she glanced over her shoulder very quickly, but her eyes were able to take in the situation fully. Then she spun back around and stared straight ahead. Her mouth had dropped open. What she'd seen was this: Becky Moss was now sitting alone in the back seat. And

Ben Ekhart was sitting next to Christinia, who for the first time in a long time was smiling.

Once Figgrotten was outside on the rocks, waiting for the crows, she put it all together. Becky had liked Ben too and had tried to claim him (or maybe even steal him), but it now looked as if Ben had rejected Becky and chosen Christinia.

Figgrotten didn't like any of it. She didn't like Becky. She didn't like Ben. And she hated Christinia. The whole thing made her dread being in eighth grade. It seemed there was a lot of meanness happening in middle school.

The fact was, she didn't know who Christinia was anymore. She knew she was a good student; she knew she was a fast runner and a good guitar player. She'd started playing guitar last year, and lately Figgrotten could hear her often in the next room playing. But suddenly, as she sat there on the rocks and looked down at the house, it occurred to her that Christinia was actually now pretty as well. Maybe even more than pretty. Maybe she was even beautiful. And Figgrotten hadn't ever really thought this before. It was as if she'd never really *seen* Christinia, because she'd seen her so much. But now, thinking of Ben choosing her to be his girlfriend made Figgrotten view her sister in another light.

She pictured her long shining dark hair, her big brown eyes, her long legs. This made Figgrotten feel jealous, and she hadn't felt all that jealous of Christinia before. She looked down at her wool coat and boots and a feeling of unhappiness came over her. Suddenly her clothing seemed old and weird.

At the dinner table that night, Christinia was not her usual miserable self. In fact, she was acting sort of cheerful to both their mom and dad. None of that mattered to Figgrotten; the wall of ice between her and Christinia still stood. Their eyes never met and they never spoke a word to each other. Figgrotten had heard the term *cold war* a bunch of times, and she could only imagine this was what that was. No explosions. Just ice. Ice and coldness between them.

At the end of the meal, instead of stomping off up to her room, Christinia stayed and helped clear the table. "That's so nice of you, sweetie," her mom said to her, looking a bit baffled.

Figgrotten made a face like she was going to be sick. Christinia was acting like an angel because stupid Ben Ekhart had sat with her on the bus?

Figgrotten left the kitchen, and now it was her stomping up the stairs and into her room. She even shut her bedroom door so forcefully that it slammed, shaking the branches that leaned near it.

She stomped around the room for a bit, then finally plopped down on the floor and opened up one of the volumes of her encyclopedia that was sitting nearby. It was the one that went from the letters *P* through *R*, and she started at the beginning and turned the pages slowly. She sat the way James Barren sat, hanging over the book, shutting the world away. She read about the painter Pablo Picasso, and about the razor-sharp teeth of piranhas, and then, most fascinating of all, she read all about Pompeii, the city in Italy that was buried underneath the ash of a humongous volcano. She'd heard about Pompeii before, but she'd never really known that people were found in the exact positions they were in when they had died. Doing the laundry, taking baths, walking down the street. "Oh wow," Figg-rotten heard herself say out loud. "Wow." She decided she needed to get a whole book just about Pompeii and all the stuff archaeologists found when they uncovered the place.

So, luckily, when she went to bed, she was no longer thinking about Christinia being prettier than her or having a stupid boyfriend. Her mind had switched over to many other more interesting thoughts and ideas, and when she fell asleep she was putting together a list in her mind of all the things she could talk to Alvin about on Monday morning.

CHAPTER NINE

But she didn't even get to go out and wait for the bus Monday morning before she knew something was wrong. She was standing in the doorway, still cradling Clark in her arms and scratching under his chin, when she heard the bus coming around the bend, five minutes earlier than usual. The gears were grinding and the bus was going much faster than usual and right away she knew Alvin was not driving it. Alvin was a slow and steady driver. A feeling of panic started coming up through her stomach.

A few seconds later, when the bus came roaring into view, Figgrotten could see through the windshield that she had been right. The bus pulled up, the door opened, and Figgrotten stood looking up at the driver. It was a tall, skinny woman with dyed-red hair.

"Where's Alvin?" Figgrotten asked, her voice coming out super high and panicky sounding.

"Beats me. I just got the four a.m. call. Climb on, girly. Got to get this route over with so I don't get canned from my regular job."

Figgrotten climbed up the steps slowly but she was thinking that maybe she shouldn't. Maybe she should run back inside and tell her mother that she needed to find out where Alvin was. But before she knew it, the door had shut and the bus was rolling and Figgrotten was thrown into her seat.

Only after they'd rounded the bend and were hurtling into town did she remember about Christinia, who hadn't been lucky enough to hear the early arrival and had missed the bus. But it didn't matter. Nothing mattered other than Alvin was not there. And she had a terrible sinking feeling about it.

When she got into her classroom, she didn't know what to do. Somehow telling Mr. Stanley didn't seem right. He didn't know Alvin or know about their friendship. So she sat down and started staring at the clock, counting the minutes until she could get back on the bus. Alvin had to be there to drive her home. Then everything would be all right.

She barely heard a word of what Mr. Stanley was talking about all morning, nor was she able to answer any of the questions he asked her. She didn't even care that James answered practically every question, sometimes without even raising his hand. Her eyes stayed on the clock.

But at the end of the day, as she was rushing to get ready to leave, Mr. Stanley said, "Frances, would you mind sticking around for a second?"

Figgrotten sat back in her chair and waited for the rest of the kids to leave the room, and she almost started crying. She wanted to race out to the bus.

Mr. Stanley was wearing a bright orange shirt and a blue bow tie, which was normal for him; he always looked super bright and sharp.

"Now, Frances," he said, walking over to her desk. "I know something was really bothering you today."

Figgrotten just sat looking down at the floor. She could feel her heart thumping in her chest. First she shrugged, then she took in a breath and said quietly, "Mr. Stanley, do you know Alvin Turkson, our bus driver?"

"Yes, of course. I know he was having heart trouble yesterday, and I believe he's in the hospital."

"He's what?" Figgrotten's voice barely came out as she gasped.

"Yes, this is what I've heard. I'm sorry you didn't know, Frances. He's a friend of yours?"

Figgrotten nodded and her eyes filled with tears. "People can die from their heart being bad," she whispered.

Mr. Stanley came over to her desk. "Frances, honestly, I don't know how Alvin is doing. He could be on his way home for all I know. So don't jump to any conclusions. I'm very sorry. I didn't know you were worried about him."

"He's my good friend—he's actually like my best friend," Figgrotten managed to say, though she had started to cry and her voice was breaking.

"Ah, well, that explains a great deal. Well . . . let me think for a second." He still had his hand on her shoulder, and she could tell he was doing what he did when he was thinking. He was gazing upward.

"How about this," he now said. "Let me go and call your mom and see if there's any way we can go visit Alvin this afternoon. Or at least find out how he is. I do think it's better to know the facts than to let yourself wonder. Let's see what your mom thinks. I'll be back in a bit."

She heard his shoes click off down the hall. The bus was probably about to leave and she was going to miss it. But nothing mattered anymore. Alvin was in the hospital.

Several minutes later Mr. Stanley came back down the hall. "Your mom agrees. She thinks it's a good idea. So instead of you getting on the bus today, I will drive you to Fairview Hospital and your mom will meet us there. Does that sound good?"

Figgrotten could only nod. But it didn't sound good. The fact was, she was terrified to see Alvin sick in the hospital.

Mr. Stanley's car was as neat and tidy as he was. There was his mint gum that fit perfectly in the little compartment by the gearshift. There was a filled bottle of water in the cup holder, and there seemed to be a steady stream of jazzy music playing at a low volume over the radio.

The car zipped along and Mr. Stanley shifted gears very quickly and smoothly.

Mr. Stanley seemed different once they pulled out onto the main road. He let out a big breath and looked over at her. "So, tell me a little about Alvin, Frances. I don't know him well. He's an unusual character, though, isn't he?"

"Well," Figgrotten said, "he reads so many books every week and knows about everything. Not just about stuff, but he's smart about people too. And the world, you know. Like, life."

"Ah," Mr. Stanley said. "He sounds rather remarkable."

"Yes," Figgrotten said quietly, but none of it was right. Alvin was impossible to describe. He was . . . just . . . Alvin. Unlike anyone else. "He goes to the library like every day and always has a new book that he reads during his free time. He's just . . . he's just such a nice person too."

Her stomach began to ache. The knot was back. And it was worse than it had ever been. She was scared.

When they pulled up to the traffic light on the main street, Figgrotten looked out and scanned the trees until her eyes landed on two crows sitting up in the naked branches. Somehow she needed to see them right then. So she homed in on them, watched them looking down at the ground, and then saw one open its mouth and make several caws.

A few minutes later, Mr. Stanley put his blinker on and they turned in to the hospital parking lot.

Figgrotten felt her stomach tighten further. After they found a space and Mr. Stanley turned off his car, she didn't move. She was biting her fingernails and staring through the windshield.

"Hospitals are nerve-racking," Mr. Stanley said.

"What if he doesn't want to see me?"

"You can wait outside with your mom and I'll go in to see if he's taking visitors. Don't worry. I think it's good we're here."

Figgrotten's mom pulled up in the spot next to them and waved at Figgrotten through the window. She looked worried and sad. Her glasses were up on her head, and her hair was a little messier than usual. She climbed out of her car and took Figgrotten's hand and they walked into the building. Figgrotten had only been in the hospital once before, when she needed a blood test because her mom was worried she had been bitten by a tick. She'd been littler then but the smell of the place brought it back immediately. The smell was very strong and Figgrotten couldn't quite make out what it was, but unfortunately it smelled a bit like pee.

Mr. Stanley asked at the front desk where Alvin Turkson's room was, and the lady looked on her computer and told him, "Room five forty-three. Take the elevator to the fifth floor and then take a right and you'll see the nurses' station." They turned and looked for the elevator, which was directly behind them.

Figgrotten kept holding her mom's hand on the elevator ride up while Mr. Stanley and her mother chatted about the cold weather. But she was thinking about Alvin. When the doors opened onto the fifth floor, Figgrotten's mother had to tug a little at her hand to get her to walk.

Mr. Stanley, as always, took the lead and walked briskly up to the nurses' station. "We were wondering if Mr. Turkson, in room five forty-three, is taking visitors at the moment."

The nurse sitting behind the desk was less friendly than the woman downstairs, and she looked up slowly at Mr. Stanley and then called over her shoulder, "Brenda, is room five forty-three awake?"

Brenda, who was very large and leaning on the counter chatting with a bunch of other nurses, leaned back and looked into one of the nearby rooms and said, "Uh, I think so." Then she went back to chatting.

Mr. Stanley glanced at Figgrotten's mom, then shrugged. "I suppose that's a yes. Let me go in and see Alvin first and make sure he's up for a visit."

Figgrotten and her mom went and sat down in the

dingy waiting room. There was a coffee table with tattered old magazines piled on it. The whole place was airless and just plain awful, as far as Figgrotten was concerned. It was about as opposite of the out-of-doors as you could get.

"I don't like it here," Figgrotten said to her mom.

Her mom sighed. "I know what you mean. But when you need the place . . ."

"Mommy, is Alvin going to die?" This finally burst out of her. She'd been too scared to ask before, but now she had to know before she went in to see him.

"Oh, Frances, Alvin is very old. I really don't know when he's going to die, but he is old and heart trouble isn't good in an old person. But there's plenty of heart trouble that can be treated. So I really just don't know."

A few minutes later Mr. Stanley came down the hall and said, "Well, he's very, very pleased you're here, Frances."

"He is?"

"Very pleased. He wants you to go in and see him. Your mother and I can wait here or we can go with you. Either way."

"I don't want to go alone," Figgrotten said.

"Fine, we'll all go. You'll see, it'll be fine."

Even though she now felt sweaty, she kept on her

hat and brown wool coat and got up and followed her mother and Mr. Stanley to room 543. When they got there, the two grown-ups stood to the side and let Figgrotten go first. She stepped into the little room and the very first thing she saw was Alvin's Greek fisherman's hat sitting on the bureau across from the bed. And when she turned and looked at him, it was worse than she had imagined. For there he was, looking tinier then he'd ever looked before, propped on a pillow. If she could have turned and fled, she would have. But her feet were already there in front of his bed, like two blocks of concrete dumped onto the floor.

"It's that bad?" Alvin said. His voice sounded gargly, like he needed to cough up some junk. "You look as scared as a cat just seen a coyote."

Figgrotten took a shaky breath in. "Are you better, Alvin?"

"Oh, I surely am. Surely. But I'm old as the hills, don't forget. Now, can you do me a favor, Miss Pauley? You see that book over there by the window? Could you bring that over to me? I've been thirsting for that ever since they took it away from me last night."

Figgrotten picked up the book. It was a library book with a plastic cover. "Why'd they take it?" she asked.

"Well, they don't know that that book is my lifeline.

They just think it's a book, and it was in their way when they were doing something to me, so they put it over there."

Figgrotten handed him the book and he took it and sighed happily and held it against his chest. If he couldn't cross the room to pick up the book, then he surely couldn't drive the school bus, Figgrotten thought with a sinking heart.

"I'm very happy you came to see me. So, now tell me, my friend, how are those birds of yours? And how's your sister? You see, I have lots of questions. Sit down right there and talk to me." He pointed with his bony hand at the chair next to his bed. She knew his hands well from seeing them hold the steering wheel for years, and they looked different now. Smoother and thinner. He'd been in the hospital for only a day, but he looked so different. "I have a clogged-up throat, so you'll need to do some of the talking."

"Um . . ." Figgrotten still hadn't moved and she was trying to unwrinkle her brow, which she could feel was all scrunched up with worry. Alvin needed to shave; his beard had come in in patches, which gave his whole face a grayish color. And the smell of pee was now worse.

"Sit," he said again.

Figgrotten took a breath and sat down in the chair. She only wanted to talk about him. To ask him if he was going to get all better. But she knew that was not what he wanted.

"Well, um, the crows still don't come when I whistle," she said.

"Time," Alvin said in his watery voice. "I bet they will learn."

"And as for my sister, she's okay, I guess. We don't get along too well." Figgrotten paused and took a breath. She could never have said this to him on the bus. But here she was, telling him this now. He wanted to hear more, as he was looking at her inquisitively. "Oh, and there was a substitute bus driver this morning. Alvin, she was terrible."

Alvin was now looking up at the ceiling, thinking. His hands were folded together on his chest and he kept nodding.

"I think you should read some Barry Lopez books," he suddenly said. "He writes about nature. I think you'd like him. And then when you get older, you can read a little Thoreau. Now, as for your sister, she's experiencing the world in a different way than you. That is plain to the naked eye. But here's what I say: Never forget that everyone needs plenty of understanding. Just as you do. And as I do. People are very different, but they are very, very similar too. Everyone has one of these." Alvin used one of his hands to thump at his heart.

He stopped and coughed a little, then turned and gazed out the window. Figgrotten could see his eyes take on a distant look. "I like to think of you up in your rock world, Miss Pauley. Now, that is a thought that I have always enjoyed."

Then he turned and looked at her, smiled, and gave his head a little nod. He reached out his hand to her and Figgrotten took it. It was so smooth and small but it wasn't warm. It was nearly icy. "Oh, Miss Pauley," he said.

Then he took his hand back and clasped it again over his book on his chest and closed his eyes. Figgrotten sat on the edge of her chair. She wasn't sure what to do now. Finally she whispered, "Alvin?" but Alvin lay there with his mouth cracked open a little and his breath pulling in sharply and letting go in big tough-sounding gusts.

From behind her, Figgrotten's mom whispered, "He must be tired, Frances. He needs to rest. I think we should probably go. We can come back again."

Figgrotten stood looking down at Alvin. "Okay,"

she said. Then she crossed the room, picked up his hat, and brought it back over to his bed. Very quietly she placed it next to him on the pillow. She knew he'd want that with him too.

She leaned and read the title on the spine of the book and whispered out loud to herself, *"The Poems of William Shakespeare."*

"I'll talk to you later, Alvin," she said, and stood for a minute looking at him before she turned and followed her mom out of the room.

Mr. Stanley was out in the hall, leaning against the wall, when they came out, and the three of them walked down the hall together. This time no one said anything.

When she got home that afternoon, she could barely whistle as she dumped out the bread crumbs for the crows. She sat down shivering on her rock and stared into the woods. Mr. Stanley had been right, it was better to know than to let your mind wonder. She now knew that when the bus came to pick her up tomorrow, Alvin would not be there pulling open the door and smiling at her. But knowing wasn't easy either. Knowing made her pull her hat down even lower than usual, almost over her eyes, so she couldn't look out, she could only look down at her feet and her knapsack, which, today, she didn't have the heart to open.

CHAPTER TEN

For the next few days, when she thought about Alvin there in the hospital, she felt panicked and miserable. She tried to distract herself by focusing extra hard on her homework, but her mind kept going back to him lying there in that bed, looking so thin and fragile.

And the substitute bus driver, Mrs. Schlosser, just made it worse. Not only was she a lousy driver given to going too fast and grinding the gears constantly, she was also irritable and short-tempered. She kept pulling the bus over to the side of the road and turning around and hollering with a beet-red face, "You better sit down in the back or we're not going anywhere!" Little did she know this was not a threat to the kids in the back. Not going anywhere meant not going to school, which was music to their ears. Figgrotten did not care either way.

She would use these moments to turn in her seat and see that Ben Ekhart was now always seated quietly next to Christinia. They both looked as awkward as could be, sitting there not talking to each other. But again, Figgrotten couldn't have cared less. She turned and sat staring out the window, aware that James was sitting behind her with his head in his stupid book. But he didn't matter. There was only one thing that mattered. Alvin.

"Is there any news?" she kept asking her mom. "Can't you call someone and see if he's better?"

So her mom did call Alvin's friend Madeleine Stroble, the librarian at the Preston Public Library, and asked if she knew anything. Madeleine said there was no new news. Alvin was still weak and still in the hospital.

"If I don't hear anything else in the next couple of days, I'll drive back over and try to see how he is," her mom told her.

At night, in bed, Figgrotten found herself again clutching her hands together under her chin. Not praying. But hoping. Hoping with everything she had that Alvin was going to be okay.

During the day, in the classroom, she stared out the window and made little bets with herself. *If I see a crow fly through the sky, I'll know Alvin is going to be fine.* And always, if she watched the sky for long enough, a crow would indeed fly into view and she'd let go a big breath of air that she hadn't even known she was holding, and for a few moments she'd feel relieved until it wore off and she went back to worrying.

On Friday Mr. Stanley took everyone in the classroom for a "speed walk" around the perimeter of the school building. He did this to define the word *perimeter* but also, as he put it, to "shake things up" because he felt like everyone in the class was getting "slouchy." Figgrotten normally loved a nice fast walk out in the fresh air, but today she fell to the back of the group and plodded along. Her feet felt heavy, as if she was wearing boots filled with water. Mr. Stanley, who had been in the lead, slowed down and waited for her to catch up to him. Then he just walked along beside her. He didn't ask her how she was. She knew he knew.

When they arrived back in the classroom, Mr. Stanley clapped his hands and said, "Okay, folks, now we're going to make a few changes in our seating." There was a loud groan from pretty much everyone, Figgrotten included. She was very attached to her seat by the window, and the idea of giving it up practically made her teary.

"First off," Mr. Stanley said, "let's rearrange the chesks so that we're in a circle for a change. Then I'll let you know who sits where." *Chesks* was Mr. Stanley's word for the chairs with the desks attached.

The kids reluctantly moved their chesks into a big circle, which was a horribly loud and screechy process. Then Mr. Stanley got out a piece of paper that he had written on already and pointed out where each assigned seat was. Figgrotten was, in fact, no longer next to the window, but at least she didn't have her back to the window and could see out. She was seated next to Fiona and Gordie, and when she plopped down in her seat the feeling of misery grew inside her. She hated this. Hate, hate, hated it. She liked being over by the window, where she was alone. Where she could drift off and no one would really notice. Here she was being looked at by everyone *and* she now had to look right back at them. And, of course, it was her luck that directly across from her was James. Wearing his army jacket, slumped down deep in his seat, keeping his eyes to the ground. She loved Mr. Stanley, but she didn't like that he had done this.

Mr. Stanley handed back everyone's two-paragraph essays on the word *civilization.* Figgrotten had written hers last week up on the rocks. It had been the part of the homework that day that she had liked the most. Hers had started out, "Without civilization, there would be a lot of fighting."

Now she looked down at her paper and turned it over and read on the back Mr. Stanley's perfect writing. It said, "As always, Frances, you've reached deep here and you've expressed many interesting thoughts, but I think you can go even further next time around, bringing all the different ideas into more of a focused ending. But, good job."

Figgrotten felt herself frowning. She worried that Mr. Stanley hadn't liked what she'd written.

Then Mr. Stanley said, "Now, everyone, I decided to choose one essay to read aloud to everyone, as I think it works in many ways."

And he began to read.

Figgrotten didn't look up. Nor did she listen.

She kept her eyes on her own essay so she wouldn't have to see that it was, of course, James's essay that was not on the desk in front of him but rather in Mr. Stanley's hand, being read out loud in a voice Figgrotten recognized. A voice that was pleased and impressed and that, in the past, Mr. Stanley had used only for her work.

This was definitely the very worst week of Figgrotten's life. She could feel she was barely holding herself together at the moment. If she so much as ventured to think about Alvin, she knew she was going to break down and start crying.

But luckily, when Mr. Stanley was done reading and had turned around, Figgrotten heard something next to her that snapped her from her bad mood. It was a puff of breath released by Fiona. It was a sound of exasperation that normally no one would be able to hear, but Figgrotten heard it, all right. It was a sound she would have liked to have made herself but hadn't. She glanced sideways just in time to see Fiona look at her and roll her eyes. And suddenly Figgrotten knew she was not alone. Fiona felt like she did. James was the star student now, and it was hard to take.

But the amazingly wonderful thing was what Figgrotten felt happen right there and then. Just from that tiny exchange, it was as if a little bridge had formed between her and Fiona. Figgrotten felt something light up inside her. And when she put away her paper, she realized suddenly she was not thinking about James or even Alvin; she was thinking about Fiona, and she was almost smiling.

She was still thinking about all this later that afternoon when she plopped into her seat on the school bus behind the dumpy dumb Mrs. Schlosser and turned to look out the window.

In fact, she was still lost in these thoughts several minutes later, when she suddenly realized that all the chatter on the bus had stopped and everyone was silent. Figgrotten looked up and saw Mrs. Flynn, the principal, standing at the top of the steps in front of everyone. The principal never came on the bus unless the kids were in big trouble. For being too rowdy, too loud, or whatever—always something bad. Mrs. Flynn was wearing her usual tweed jacket and skirt and her usual blue eye shadow that looked a bit smudged, but today she didn't have the irritated expression that Figgrotten had seen her with so often.

"Girls and boys," Mrs. Flynn said in a kind voice, one that Figgrotten did not recognize. "I have some sad news to deliver to you all." Figgrotten felt something inside her body drop. As if her whole stomach just fell right down onto the floor. Then she was flooded with a horrible panicked feeling. "Your bus driver, Alvin Turkson, passed away this morning in Fairview Hospital. He was eighty-three years old." Mrs. Flynn paused and took a breath. Then, very slowly, she shook her head. "Imagine that. He drove this bus for over thirty years, and really, until this week, when he became ill, he barely missed a day. I know you all were very fond of him. It is never easy to say goodbye to a friend. We've just called and also sent an email out to all of your parents. So please, go home and talk to them about your feelings. Monday in school, we'll gather and do more of the same. Mr. Turkson, I know, will be greatly missed. In the meantime, Mrs. Schlosser will bring you all home. I'm terribly sorry to deliver this sad news to you all."

She turned slowly and climbed down off the bus, and the silence that followed as Mrs. Schlosser closed the door and the bus began to move was complete. Only the sound of the bus rolling out onto the road could be heard. Not one person said a word the whole drive. Not the bad kids in the back. Not the smaller kids in the front.

Figgrotten was still barely breathing. She was in the same frozen position that she had taken as soon as she knew what Mrs. Flynn was going to say. Even the words had not gone into her head. And certainly not the thought that Alvin had died. That thought was shut out like a bee trying to sting her through a piece of glass. The only thought that she had was this: *No. No. No.*

When the bus arrived at their house, Figgrotten's mom was standing on the porch in a heavy sweater, clutching her arms around herself. Figgrotten thought her mom looked like she'd maybe been crying. Christinia got off before Figgrotten and rushed up the porch steps right past her mom. She threw open the front door, and a second later Figgrotten heard her racing up the stairs. But her mom came rushing down to Figgrotten and put her arms around her and they stayed like that for a long minute.

"Oh, honey," her mom finally said. "It's just very, very sad. Alvin was such a wonderful friend."

But Figgrotten couldn't even nod. Something had locked up hard inside her.

"Frances, let's go inside and sit in the kitchen."

Figgrotten shook her head. "I have to go be on the rocks. I need to be" was all she could get out.

Her mom hugged her again.

"Okay, sweetie. I better go check on your sister. I think she's probably very upset as well."

It was the first time Figgrotten even considered that Christinia might be sad about Alvin too. After all, Alvin had been especially kind to Christinia as well for years. Even more years than he was to Figgrotten.

She walked into the house and stood at the bottom of the stairs while her mother went upstairs and into Christinia's room. She was glad the door was open a little so she could listen in.

At first there was quiet but then there was an outburst and Christinia cried out, "I didn't get to say goodbye like Frances did, Mom! Why didn't anyone tell me he was dying?"

"We didn't know, sweetie. I'm so sorry."

And then Christinia began to cry. Howling was more like it, like she was in pain, which gave Figgrotten a desperate frightened feeling and made her own throat tighten up hard so that it hurt. She turned and walked into the kitchen, grabbed the bread crumb bag her mom had left her, then went outside and up to her rocks. Though the day had started out sunny, it was now gray and gusty and cold. The wind seemed to be high up in the pine trees, and when Figgrotten closed her eyes it was the wind she heard, a soft roaring noise. She was shivering horribly, shivering more than she had ever shivered, and she sat with her arms wrapped around herself. She wasn't going to think about Alvin being dead. She could not think it. She sucked in several big gulping breaths to try to get rid of the feeling. Then she just sat for a long while staring down at her shoes and trying not to think. She felt sick and awful and terrible. And she couldn't move. But she did not shed a tear. She knew if she started crying, there was no way she could ever stop.

What felt like a long time later, she had the strange feeling she was being watched. And when she lifted her head and looked up, there they were, all four of them, high up and perched on different branches of the big pine above her. They'd come right on time. But it wasn't her whistle that was doing it, because today not only had she forgotten to whistle, she'd forgotten to put the bread out entirely.

PART TWO

CHAPTER ELEVEN

On the following Friday, seven horrible dreadful days after Alvin died, Figgrotten was sent to the principal's office for the first time in her life. Mr. Stanley actually took her there. He marched her without saying a word other than "Frances, follow me, I am taking you to Mrs. Flynn." And down the hall they went, Mr. Stanley with his shoes clicking sharply and Figgrotten following behind with her cheeks on fire. It wasn't humiliation that made them hot this time. It was fury.

It was the end of a very strange week. On Monday everyone who rode on bus number 8, Alvin's bus, had

had to go to the cafeteria for a group session with the school psychologist. That had been downright terrible, because Figgrotten felt like everyone was looking at her the whole time, knowing Alvin was her best friend. And as sad as they were, they all knew that she was sadder. But the fact was, she didn't feel sadder. She just felt angry that Alvin had been taken away from her. So instead of sad, she felt mean.

The psychologist's name was Mr. Hammer, and he was short and bald, and the minute Figgrotten laid eyes on him she decided she didn't like him. He was the kind of person who pretended he understood everyone around him, including her.

"Let's start by talking about Alvin Turkson, kids. Who would like to say something about him? Anyone."

The group was dead quiet, and when Figgrotten glanced up, sure enough, everyone seemed to be staring at her.

"Okay, well, let me get you all started, then. Tell me a little about Alvin. Was he a kind person?"

Everyone nodded and agreed that he was very nice.

Figgrotten did not move.

"Was he funny?"

There were then a lot of shrugs.

Figgrotten did not move.

"Was he smart?"

"He liked to read," Ben Ekhart suddenly said. Ben was sitting next to Christinia and across the table from Figgrotten. "He read a lot. He was more than just regularly smart."

This made Figgrotten lift her eyes briefly and she was surprised that his eyes met hers. She'd always considered Ben just one of the unruly boys from the back of the bus, but that changed right there and then because the look he gave her was the kind of look a friend gives you. A knowing look. A look of camaraderie.

"Alvin was a genius," Christinia added. "He knew everything."

Figgrotten glanced up and saw that Christinia was looking at her. She didn't have her usual angry expression on her face. She just looked sad. This made Figgrotten suddenly feel like she could easily start to cry.

"Did any of you ever worry he might be so old he might die?"

Again there was a lot of shrugging and shaking of heads.

"In some religions, when someone you know dies, you really make sure you mourn their loss. You make sure, every day, that you think of them and spend some special time remembering them, missing them and grieving for them. I'm not telling you all that you should do this. I'm just telling you that in many parts of the world, this is done. And I think it's not a terrible idea. Because otherwise you can have sad feelings for a long time about all this and really not even know it."

Suddenly Figgrotten put her hand up and every single person turned to look at her, interested to hear what she was going to add.

"I have to go to the bathroom," she said.

"Oh." Mr. Hammer seemed a little startled. "Well, by all means, go."

At which point Figgrotten stood up, walked out of the cafeteria, went into the girls' room, and leaned against the wall next to the sink for fifteen whole minutes, and when she came back out, to her great relief the meeting about Alvin was over.

That was on Monday. On Thursday morning Mrs. Schlosser, the substitute bus driver, was replaced by the new permanent bus driver, and he was far worse than anything Figgrotten could have dreamed up. He was round and pimply and he wore a fluorescent orange hunting hat, and the first thing Figgrotten thought about him was that he was stupid. They had replaced Alvin with someone dumb. And from the minute he pushed open the door and grunted, she absolutely couldn't stand to look at him.

Then came Friday. Friday was when Fiona, in her mouse voice, attempted to answer a question in class. Mr. Stanley had asked if a preposition went before a verb or after. And Fiona had raised her hand and was just beginning to talk when James, who also had his hand up, burst out with the answer and drowned her out. The worst part of this was that Mr. Stanley didn't seem to notice.

"That's correct, James." Mr. Stanley said, and began to explain further the role of prepositions in a sentence. And Figgrotten could hear the air go out of the mouse next to her. It wasn't exasperated huffy air like before. It was Fiona's spirit deflating.

And that, at the end of the worst week of her life, was when Figgrotten finally lost it.

First her face felt super hot; then she stood up out of her chair and started shouting at Mr. Stanley. "WHY DON'T YOU STOP HIM? HE DOESN'T GIVE ANYONE ELSE A CHANCE TO ANSWER. WHY DON'T YOU DO ANYTHING?"

At first a deadly silence fell over the classroom.

Then there was a sniffle, which came from Fiona, who suddenly stood up and ran out of the room.

And then the worst part was, James stood up and rushed out of the room as well. His eyes were red and Figgrotten had a sinking feeling that he too might have started crying.

At which point Mr. Stanley told the class not to make a sound and stay in their seats and he said, "Frances Pauley, come with me this instant. We are going to the principal's office."

Mr. Stanley left Figgrotten alone in the waiting area of the principal's office while he went in and spoke privately with Mrs. Flynn. Then he came out and told Figgrotten she could go in and he walked back toward the classroom. Figgrotten stood up slowly and went into Mrs. Flynn's office and sat down on the chair in front of her desk.

Mrs. Flynn didn't seem all that upset with Figgrotten. Clearly she was used to troublemakers, and Figgrotten, in comparison, was a lightweight case.

"So, Mr. Stanley tells me you lost your temper in the classroom, Frances."

Figgrotten nodded and looked down at her hands, which were holding on to each other in her lap. "James is ruining our class," she said quietly. "He thinks he knows it all."

"Well," the principal said in a tight, impatient voice,

"that is Mr. Stanley's business, not yours. Do you understand, young lady?"

Figgrotten nodded. Her anger had fallen away and she felt deflated.

"Fine, then. I don't want to hear another word about it. You may go back to your classroom now."

Luckily, when Figgrotten got back to the classroom, everyone was in the Art Room, so she didn't have to walk back in with people looking at her. She hated being stared at more than anything else. She went and sat down at her desk and gazed miserably across the room.

A minute later Mr. Stanley came in and saw her. He stopped, furrowed up his eyebrows at her, then let go of a big breath. "Everything is a lesson, Frances. Things that bother you and make you angry and make you sad. And the lesson is just this: how to make it through life without hurting yourself or hurting anyone else." He walked over to his desk and shuffled through his stacks; then he sat down and began correcting papers.

Figgrotten sat without moving for a minute, then she said, "I'm sorry, Mr. Stanley. Very sorry."

Mr. Stanley looked up at her. "I know you are, Frances. It's okay." His voice had softened back into its usual tone. "I do wish you had come to me about all that with James. He'd had a really hard go in his last class, and I guess I was allowing him to take the lead because I was worried about squelching him. So I too am sorry, Frances. I realize it's been a truly difficult week for you. However, it's important you take care of your sad feelings so they don't erupt elsewhere, like today. Now, can we start over and move on and just forget this happened? However, I of course expect you to apologize to James."

She sat and looked out the window. She wished Mr. Stanley hadn't taken her to the principal's office. It felt starkly apparent suddenly that he was, after all, just her teacher, not her friend. A wonderful, brilliant teacher. But he wasn't like Alvin had been, nor would he ever be. Alvin would not have ever marched her to the principal's office. He would have understood her. This thought deepened her already horribly lonely feelings.

It was not even twenty degrees out, which meant indoor recess. This, as far as Figgrotten was concerned, was ludicrous. Fifteen degrees was nearly perfect, not something dangerous. It was probably a rule that Mrs. Flynn made up. Just like keeping the kids out of the woods.

Most kids went down to the gym and screamed and ran around. Other kids stood around in the commons and talked. Others watched a movie. Figgrotten went into the library and walked around looking at books. She found one on anthropology that she'd never seen before, and she sat down on the floor, cross-legged, and opened the book and slowly began turning the pages. There were a lot of photographs of tribes of people. People in Africa and Australia and New Guinea. Figgrotten was more interested in the faces of these people than anything else about the book. They all seemed to have a bit of the same expression. It wasn't happy or smiling or crying or angry. She sat squinting and thinking. It was as if each person was thinking only about the camera and nothing else. Maybe, from the looks of it, they didn't know what a photograph even was.

Suddenly Figgrotten heard giggling coming from nearby and she looked up and there were the two bully girls, the same ones from the bathroom the day when she went home early.

"Oh, gag," one of them said. "What is that on the floor?"

They were talking about her and she knew it. Figgrotten went back to looking at the book, but her heart was racing hard in her chest.

The other girl whispered to the first one and they fell against each other in a heap of hysterics. Figgrotten was aware that she had just been sent to the principal's office for screaming at the top of her lungs, so she knew she couldn't do that again. Besides, she felt so furious she couldn't think clearly. She couldn't even see the book that she was pretending to look at now. She sucked in a breath and sat horribly still.

The giggling kept on for another minute; then it stopped abruptly and she heard someone walking toward where she was sitting. She realized it was a boy because she saw his black sneakers. He squatted down and seemed to be searching the bookshelves right next to her. He was humming under his breath but she could tell it was fake humming. It was the kind of humming you do when you're pretending to be busy. Figgrotten imagined reaching out her arm and slugging him, whoever he was, because she was sure he was in on the joke with the two other girls. But then, when he pulled out a book and said under his breath, "Those two ugly dorks are gone now," she realized he was on her side. Only then did she glance through her hair, which was hanging down over her face, and see him as he stood and walked away. It was Ben Ekhart.

That afternoon, for the first time in her life, Figgrotten didn't sit up in the front seat of the bus. She got on and, without so much as a glance at the new stupid pimply driver with the orange hunting hat, marched to the third seat from the back and plunked down. She heard one kid in the back seat make an "Ooh" sound at her, but she hunkered in close to the window and stared out and did not acknowledge it. She hadn't planned on sitting back there, but when she stepped onto the bus, that same sickly sad feeling had come over her at the thought of sitting in her regular seat right behind where Alvin should be, so instead she'd just kept walking. Now, as she watched the kids pour out of the doors, she could feel her heart thumping in her chest. "Change," Mr. Stanley had said many times in the past, "is good for everyone." But the change really was Alvin being gone forever, and that, as far as Figgrotten could see, was just plain terrible.

A few minutes later Ben and Christinia climbed on and sat down two seats in front of Figgrotten. She kept her face turned toward the window for fear of meeting a nasty look from Christinia. But when she took a quick glance, she saw that Christinia didn't actually look angry at all. For the second time since Alvin died, Figgrotten saw something in her sister's expression that was more like sadness than anything else. Figgrotten frowned and turned back to the window. Her promise to not speak to Christinia again was set down hard inside her. It was like a big old block of concrete, cold and unmoving.

Once they were seated, Figgrotten found herself studying the back of Ben's head. He wore a wool hat that poked up a bit on top of his head, which Figgrotten liked because she thought it looked sort of funny.

When at last the bus lurched out of the school lot, she breathed a sigh of relief: no one had sat down next to her. This would be her new seat. She'd have to endure a few rides to establish that it was hers, but the first step, she was certain, was the hardest. It wasn't happiness that she felt as she looked out the window. It was more the feeling you have when you finish something you've been putting off forever. It was relief, she realized.

CHAPTER TWELVE

On *Saturday morning*, a week before Alvin's memorial service was to be held at the library in town, Mrs. Pauley leaned into Figgrotten's room and said, "Fiona Peterson's mom just called to ask if you'd like to go to their house today."

Figgrotten, who was still in bed, scowled. "No way," she said, then went back down under her covers and pulled the sheets up over her head.

She heard her mother sigh. After that there was a long silence, which worried her. It meant, most likely, that her mom was angry at her. She knew her mom didn't like it when she acted antisocial, like when she was reluctant to go to birthday parties. And then, a few seconds later, when she heard the tone of her mother's voice, she knew she was indeed mad. "Get dressed, Frances. You're going." She didn't exactly slam the door, but she didn't shut it delicately either.

Figgrotten sat for a long time not moving. Whenever she was told she had to do something in that way, something inside her turned into a lump of concrete and she couldn't move. She knew what this was—it was stubbornness—but there was nothing she could do about it. Her mom had pointed it out to her many times. (When she'd told her she needed a new coat was an example of this.) But finally Figgrotten got out of bed, and very, very slowly she got herself dressed. If you could call it that. She kept her flannel pj pants on and put her boots on right over them.

Figgrotten didn't believe for a minute that Fiona had wanted her to come over to her house. She knew it was coming from Fiona's mother. Mrs. Peterson must have heard about the screaming incident and somehow must have thought Figgrotten was Fiona's friend. Or something. Who knew? All Figgrotten knew was that her morning plans were now ruined. She'd wanted to spend the entire day up on the rocks, out in the bright cold air.

Alone. But now she had to go over to Fiona's house and she didn't want to.

She'd only been on a few playdates in her life, and she'd pretty much hated them all. First, they were inside, and that was one huge problem. Second, she didn't have anything in common with the girls who'd invited her over. They had mostly played with dolls, and although she had nothing against dolls, they always had bored her. The girls also liked things on TV that Figgrotten didn't. Cartoons with high-pitched voices that were supposed to be funny but just seemed sort of dumb.

In the car on the way to Fiona's house, Figgrotten sat slumped down in her seat with a sour expression on her face. She had refused to eat breakfast and her tummy was now grumbling. And because Figgrotten had put up a fuss about going, her mother still seemed a bit mad. She drove in silence.

When they pulled into Fiona's driveway, Mrs. Peterson came out and greeted them by the car. She had brown mousy hair like Fiona's and she was wearing a thick sweater that looked like she had made it herself.

"Hi, Frances, Fiona is so happy that you wanted to come over. You can go in the house, she's inside. I'll just chat with your mom for a minute about getting you home later."

Figgrotten shuffled along the walk to Fiona's front door. They lived in a tiny little house that looked hot even from the outside. She climbed the concrete steps and looked through the glass door. Fiona was standing there looking out at Figgrotten. It surprised Figgrotten to see that she looked almost as miserable as Figgrotten felt. Fiona pushed the door open and held it so Figgrotten could step inside.

"Hi," she said.

"Hi," Figgrotten replied, looking around. The place was very tidy.

"What do you want to do?" Fiona said in her little wispy voice.

Figgrotten shrugged.

"Do you want to see my room?"

Figgrotten shrugged again and followed Fiona down a short hallway. Her room was as boring as she was. There was a lot of pink stuff. Pink bedspread, pink walls, pink curtains. And there were pictures of horses all over the place and a few pictures of puppies that had been cut out of magazines and taped to the walls.

Figgrotten wasn't quite sure what to do next.

"Do you have any pets?" she asked.

"Just a bird."

"A real bird? Like in a cage?"

Fiona nodded and led the way back out of her room, down the hall, and into another little room, and sure enough, there was a large cage that seemed to take up half the space, and inside it was a green parrot with shiny red feathers on his tail.

"He's my mom's. She got him in college and has had him ever since. She's had him longer than she's had me. His name is Marcus."

Figgrotten had stepped up close to the cage and was staring in at the beautiful bird. He was huge, easily the size of a crow, and he was looking back at her.

"TREAT! TREAT!" he suddenly screeched very loudly, and Figgrotten stumbled back away from the cage.

Fiona started to giggle but then contained herself. "He says some words. *Treat* is his favorite one."

"He talks?" Figgrotten asked excitedly. "For real?'

"Yup. And he's thirty years old." Fiona reached into a container that was on the floor and pulled out a tiny dog biscuit. The bird stepped sideways along his bar and Fiona slipped the biscuit to him. He took it in his big hooked beak and then stepped sideways back away along the bar. Then, carefully, using his feet to hold it, he proceeded to eat it.

Figgrotten's mouth had dropped open and she stared at him. "He's incredible," she whispered.

"I love him too," Fiona said in a voice that was a little less whispery. She glanced over at Figgrotten, smiling.

"What else does he say?" Figgrotten asked.

"Um, he says, 'Hello' and 'How you?' and 'Pretty birdy.'"

At which point Marcus, who had just finished his biscuit, screeched, "PRETTY BIRDY," and again Figgrotten jumped back and both girls melted into a fit of giggles. At first Figgrotten was laughing at the bird, but then she realized she was laughing at Fiona's laugh, which was high-pitched and went up and down like a chipmunk racing along the keys of a piano. The more she laughed, the more Figgrotten laughed, and it just went on and on until Fiona's mother stuck her head in the room and said, "What's so funny?" and both the girls got hold of themselves and told Mrs. Peterson that they had no idea what was so funny.

"Can we go outside?" Figgrotten asked Fiona after they'd fed Marcus a few more biscuits.

"Sure," Fiona said. "I have a place outside you might like."

"What do you mean 'a place'?"

"A hangout. I'll show you," Fiona told her.

"Oh, I have a place outside too," Figgrotten said.

They bundled up in coats and hats and mittens and Figgrotten followed Fiona out the back door and across their yard. There was a stand of pine trees behind their garage and they walked in through the trees. There was one huge tree that had fallen halfway down, landing in the crook of another tree. Fiona climbed up on the fallen tree, then started walking on all fours, slowly balancing up along it until she was out on the branch of the other tree.

"Oh wow! You're so far up there!" Figgrotten said, and followed Fiona's lead, crawling along the first tree. "This is so great!" she said.

When she got up to where Fiona was, she sat next to her on the branch and dangled her legs. When she looked down, her breath caught a little as she realized how high up she really was.

"Wow," she said again breathlessly.

"I know," Fiona said. "My mom freaks out a bit when I come up here, but I told her I'd be super careful, so she lets me."

They sat for a bit not saying anything. Figgrotten had never thought for a minute that Fiona would have the guts to go up high in a tree like this.

"I'm sorry I got you in trouble yesterday," Fiona then said, and her voice was mousy again.

"Oh, it wasn't your fault. That was my fault. I shouldn't have yelled."

"Well," Fiona said, and then there was a long pause before she said, "But that James is such a know-it-all. I always want to yell at him. I wish he wasn't so cute."

"Cute?" Figgrotten gave Fiona a confused look. She'd never ever thought of James as cute. "Is he cute?" Figgrotten scrunched up her face.

Fiona burst into a fit of crazy high-pitched giggling and then they were both back at it, sitting up on the tree branch, unable to stop.

For lunch Fiona's mother made the girls grilled cheese sandwiches with American cheese and gave them each a bag of potato chips. Figgrotten thought she'd died and gone to heaven. They ate in the little kitchen, which Figgrotten suddenly viewed as sort of cheerful. It seemed the pink even continued outside of Fiona's room.

At one point, when Mrs. Peterson stepped out of the room, Figgrotten asked Fiona where her dad was and she shrugged.

"He doesn't live here," she told Figgrotten. "My parents are divorced. He lives in Rhode Island and I don't see him much." Figgrotten, when she heard this, didn't know what to say, so she didn't say anything. But it didn't seem like Fiona felt too terrible about her dad not being around.

After lunch Mrs. Peterson brought Figgrotten back home. Both she and Fiona rode in the backseat and didn't talk much because Mrs. Peterson was listening.

"Maybe sometime you could sleep over," Fiona's mom said to Figgrotten.

"I've never had a sleepover," Figgrotten said. "But I'd like it. As long as Fiona doesn't mind sleeping with the window open."

Both Fiona and her mom laughed at this and then Figgrotten had to laugh too because of Fiona's crazy giggling.

"Because you want to escape or because you want fresh air?" Fiona managed to ask.

"Oh, because I'm hot usually," said Figgrotten, but it was occurring to her that asking for the window open might be weird enough that she wouldn't get the invite to sleep over again, so she said, "I mean, that's just in our house, though, because the heat is always blasting. Your house was nice and I could sleep with the window closed most likely."

Fiona started up once again, and when they pulled

into Figgrotten's driveway they were both doubled over, snorting and gasping in a fit of giggles.

Later, up on the rocks, Figgrotten shook out the bread crumbs and whistled. Though she barely had to whistle anymore. It seemed the birds were always waiting there now, perched in the pine trees. They flew down almost immediately after she put the bread out. Being with Fiona had distracted her for a few hours. She'd only thought about Alvin a few times while she'd been there, and now that she was home the thought of him being gone struck her hard and fresh all over again. Her heart began aching again inside her chest, and she climbed down off the rocks. Even if she had a new friend, even if she was ever to like a boy, even if she grew up and became a famous anthropologist like Margaret Mead, nothing would ever take away the sadness she felt at no longer being able to see Alvin, her best friend. And as she thought this she felt like she was about to cry. The beginning of tears burned the corners of her eyes. So to snap herself out of it, she stepped into the kitchen and asked her dad in a funny too-high voice what he was making for dinner.

"Chicken Parmesan," her dad, who was standing at the kitchen sink, said over his shoulder. "Sound good?"

"Sounds yummy," Figgrotten said, again in a fake-cheerful voice. She sat down at the table. It had worked. The feeling that she was about to break apart had passed. It was what she would do from now on when her sadness threatened to come out. She'd reach inside herself and just snap it off.

CHAPTER THIRTEEN

But the plan didn't really work.

Early Monday morning she was sitting on the side of her bed, looking down at her feet. She'd woken up in the middle of a dream and it was still dawning on her, slowly, that it had been only that. A dream. In it Alvin was there behind the wheel of the bus and he was driving along like everything was normal. And Figgrotten was sitting in her usual seat right behind him, feeling hugely relieved that everyone had been wrong. He hadn't died after all. He was alive and he was right there where he had always been. The only thing in the dream that didn't make sense was that when Alvin pulled the door open to let one of the kids aboard, it wasn't a student who got on. It was the principal. And when Figgrotten saw her climb up the steps, she knew Mrs. Flynn was there to announce all over again that Alvin had died. And this is when she woke up with her heart beating hard in her chest. The dream felt so real it was as if she had just been with Alvin, and she sat trying to hold on to that feeling.

As she started to get dressed she felt a heaviness in her bones. While she could snap off the tears, she couldn't make the sadness go away.

When she arrived downstairs she found Christinia sitting at the table, already eating breakfast. They both had toast every morning. Two pieces each, with butter. The only difference was Figgrotten liked a heavy coating of raspberry jam on hers, while Christinia liked it plain. Mrs. Pauley had gone down into the basement to clean the cat pan, so it was just the two sisters sitting at the table together. Figgrotten took her plate of toast and put it on her lap and turned and looked out the window while she ate. This way she didn't have to face Christinia. She looked out into the trees, hoping to see the crows.

"Did you have fun at Fiona's house?" Christinia

suddenly asked behind her. Her sister's voice, which had not spoken to her for a month now, sounded different.

Figgrotten froze and stopped chewing. Christinia was trying to talk to her? Figgrotten felt something stiffen inside. Then her face, she could tell, began getting hot with anger. She turned and looked over her shoulder and glared at her sister, then put her toast back on the table and stood up and walked out of the kitchen.

A few minutes later she was waiting for the bus and her stomach was grumbling with hunger. She was not going to forgive Christinia. There was that concrete block inside her, heavy and unbudging. Whatever the opposite of forgiveness was, this was that.

When the bus came lumbering around the corner, with the lumpy pimply driver in his orange hunting hat at the wheel, Figgrotten climbed on without looking at him and walked back to her new seat. A minute later Christinia got on and Figgrotten kept herself turned toward the window so she didn't have to see her sister walk up the aisle and sit two seats in front of her, next to Ben Ekhart. But once the bus started rolling, Figgrotten could look at the backs of their heads. She saw them lean toward each other and say something and then laugh, saw that their shoulders were almost touching. She wasn't sure what to make of it all. But it made her frown and feel confused. She now at least knew Ben wasn't the terrible person she'd always thought he was, but she still thought having a boyfriend was stupid. And Christinia having a boyfriend was extra stupid.

While everyone took their math quiz later that morning, Mr. Stanley stood quietly next to the window. He had his hands clasped behind his back and he was gazing outside. Figgrotten kept glancing up at him and then going back to her math. They were working on long division, which was particularly annoying and pointless as far as Figgrotten could tell, and while she was still working on the second-to-last problem she heard someone else in the class set their pencil down and shift in their seat. She didn't have to look up to see who it was, but she did anyway: Glancing up, she saw James sit back in his chair and look around. She squinted, remembering that Fiona had referred to him as cute. Then she went back and finished the last problem. Having James finish before her made her feel defeated, like she had been in a race without knowing it and had just lost. It now occurred to her that this was how she had started feeling ever since James had come to the class.

Mr. Stanley had yet to move. He was still staring out the window, looking up into the sky, which was a clear and brilliant blue. Figgrotten looked up at him again and her head tilted a tiny bit to one side, as something in him, she thought, looked wistful.

Just then he began to speak quietly. "Once you are done," he said without turning around, still looking outside, "please put your pencils down and sit quietly and allow those who are not yet finished to continue their work."

Figgrotten folded her hands on her desk. She and James were still the only two who were finished. And a minute later she saw Fiona finish as well. She looked around at the other kids in the room, who were all still working on the quiz, and she saw that some of them were bent too far over their work. Bent so close that their elbows sprawled far out to the sides. The kids who were bent that close, she could tell, were the ones who were having the hardest time. They were throwing their whole bodies into understanding each problem. She knew this posture from years of finishing tests early. She knew the kids in her class who were always the last to finish. She had to wonder what it must be like to be one of those kids. The ones who always got tons wrong, the ones who had Mr. Stanley take their tests away before they were finished. The whole thing struck her as unfair. Why would someone who tried to learn something and had a hard time learning something not get the same test score as the people who learned it easily? Wasn't it just about trying? It was one of the many problems she had with school, like fencing off the woods. It didn't make any sense.

"Okay, folks, time's up," Mr. Stanley said, and he went around the classroom gathering up the quizzes.

Figgrotten could see some of the kids frown when Mr. Stanley took their tests from them, but once he'd collected all of them, he put them on his desk and crossed his arms over his chest and looked around the classroom. Everyone was quiet, as they could feel something was about to happen. Mr. Stanley was smiling.

"Now, people, I think you have all been working hard and I want to give you a little something. Sooooo . . . for the next hour we're going to have some fun. First, we're going to put some music on; second, we're going to all take off our shoes; third, I'll give you each a choice as to what you'd like to do. You can either draw or write poetry or write a letter to a person you know, or you can lie on a yoga mat and take a nap. In other words, you can do as you like within reason. No jumping! Okay? Sound good? Oh, you can also read if you'd like."

Mr. Stanley turned neatly around, walked over to his CD player and hit a button, and some very loud and peppy music began to play. Figgrotten had never heard this kind of music before; there was a lot of drumming and singing in a foreign language.

"Cuban music!" Mr. Stanley said, loudly, over the tunes. "Okay, all, shoes off. And sit in a big circle on the rug." Everyone kicked off their sneakers and went over to the rug. Fiona came over timidly and sat next to Figgrotten, which made Figgrotten surprisingly happy. It seemed they were now friends.

They both sat with their backs against the wall and pads of paper on their laps. Fiona began drawing a horse that was absolutely perfect. It was grazing and had a long flowing mane.

"Boy, I wish I could draw like that," Figgrotten said. "I can't even draw a stick figure."

"Yeah, but you sure write better than me," Fiona said. "I loved that poem you wrote for our Thanksgiving lunch thing. It was so good."

"Really?" Figgrotten made a scrunched-up face. She'd never thought of herself as a poet, but suddenly the idea of this made her feel good.

Figgrotten looked around the room. Her pen was poised above her paper but no words for a poem came to her. She needed to be alone to write something like a poem. Up on her rocks was the best place. It didn't feel like something you could do with people looking at you.

"Draw a doodley design," Fiona said to her. "Draw lots and lots of circles on your paper. Then fill them in with swirlies. It's fun."

And so that was exactly what Figgrotten did.

"My dad taught me how to do that," Fiona said. "He told me that if you want to think, it helps if you doodle."

The classroom was filled with chatter and excitement, but the one person who didn't seem to be having a good time was, of course, James. He sat cross-legged with the big book on his lap, reading. He didn't look up, and he let his hair hang down so that his face was hidden.

"Smarty-pants," Fiona whispered into Figgrotten's ear, looking over at James.

Figgrotten nodded, but the meanness she had felt about him seemed to not really be there anymore. Now she just wished she hadn't yelled at him and told him to shut up.

She glanced around the room at the other boys, who were wrestling on the yoga mats and getting super wild. She had to wonder who James could be friends with among the group. He wasn't like any of the other boys.

At the end of their free time, Mr. Stanley took everyone for one of his speed walks to "burn off the extra craziness." They walked to the gym, then through the big lobby, then down around the library.

Fiona and Figgrotten walked together and giggled as they sped along. It was as they were coming back down the main hallway that Ben Ekhart, who had come out of his classroom and was ambling toward the boys' room, fell into step with Figgrotten so they were walking side by side.

"Hey," he said to her. "How's it going?"

Figgrotten gave a tiny shrug because she felt too nervous to get any words out.

And for the length of the hallway, he walked beside her. Her cheeks, she knew, were glowing like two big brake lights.

"Later, gator," he said. Then he peeled away from her and ducked into the boys' room.

As soon as he was out of earshot, Fiona nearly shrieked, "Oh *wow,* he's *cute*!"

"Sister's boyfriend," Figgrotten said, trying to sound casual about it.

"Oh boy, he's, like, *so* cute!" Fiona said again, and out flew the chipmunk giggles.

And there was that word again. *Cute.* Figgrotten had never thought of any boy as cute, but Fiona seemed to know all the ones who were. This, she figured, was something she would eventually get the hang of, who was cute and who wasn't.

That night, when Figgrotten was brushing her teeth, something on the floor next to her foot caught her eye, and she bent down and picked up one of Christinia's little pink hair clips. Figgrotten held it in the palm of her hand and stared at it; then she set her toothbrush down, took the little clip, snapped it into her hair, and stepped back and looked at herself. How was it possible something as small as that could make her look so different? She unclipped it, but instead of putting it in the jar with all of Christinia's hair bands and clips, she tucked it into her pocket and finished brushing her teeth.

CHAPTER FOURTEEN

Figgrotten put her hand in the pocket of her brown coat on her way to school the next day and found the hair clip. She touched it with her fingers and felt around its little pink plastic flower. She was two seats behind Christinia and Ben. He was wearing his wool hat, gray with red stripes. But peeking out of the hat and curling onto his neck was his straggly hair. This was the part of him she liked the best. The raggedy part. The worn sneakers. The ripped jeans that hung down too low.

She looked out the window and saw they were coming up to James's house. Figgrotten leaned a little and saw

James standing alone on the sidewalk. He had his backpack on and in one hand was clutching his book. When the bus stopped, he climbed on and without looking at anyone sat down in the same seat close to the front. The pimply lumpy driver didn't even say hello to him. Alvin would have kept reaching out to James had he been there. He would have kept saying good morning to him and eventually he would have asked him what he was reading. He would have become a friend to him just like he was a friend to Figgrotten and everyone else.

But not the new driver. He just sat like a big lump in his orange hunting hat and drove the bus. Figgrotten did everything she could not to have to look at him. She kept her eyes averted. But occasionally she couldn't help herself and saw his face in the mirror. She had no worries that he would spot her scowling at him, because he never so much as glanced in the mirror. For Alvin, looking in the mirror was half the job of driving the bus. He drove and he also watched over his riders.

At recess that day Figgrotten asked Fiona if she'd help her for a minute, and they walked into the girls' room together. Figgrotten pulled out the hair clip and held it out to Fiona. "Can you put it in my hair?"

Fiona didn't look even slightly surprised at the request. "Sure," she said. "But you know you have to take off your hat." Then, after a spurt of chipmunk giggles, Fiona fiddled with the clip until it was in a perfect place. "Now do not touch it," she said, and stepped back and crossed her arms over her chest. "Hey, that looks really nice."

Figgrotten turned and looked at herself in the mirror and again felt surprised at how the little clip changed her so much. Then she stuffed her hat into her jacket pocket, took a deep breath, and walked out of the bathroom.

The only person who seemed to notice the clip was Mr. Stanley. He was correcting papers at his desk when Figgrotten walked into the classroom, and he glanced up at her and did a double take. He smiled and opened his mouth to say something but then didn't and went back to his papers. Figgrotten felt relieved. She wanted to wear the clip without a lot of attention focused on it. Just like changing seats on the bus. *Do it for a couple of days and people will get used to it.* That was her hope.

Having the clip in her hair for the rest of the day made Figgrotten feel so different she might as well have been wearing fake eyelashes for the first time. Or a dress. Luckily, other than people looking at her extra hard, no one said a thing to her about it. When she got on the bus, one of the boys gave her a funny look as she was walking up the aisle. But then, once she was in her seat, she was safe and the first day with the clip was almost over. The last worry was Christinia. Somehow this was the hardest part of all.

"I like the hair clip," Christinia said, again with her voice casual like before, when they got into the kitchen. "It looks nice. You can have it."

Figgrotten didn't say anything. She stuffed a granola bar into her coat pocket and stepped out the back door. But before she could shut it, Christinia said, "And I can show you how to do one on the other side if you want."

Figgrotten stopped for a second, but then, without answering, she shut the door.

Up on the rocks, she fished her hat out of her pocket and pulled it over her head and breathed a little sigh of relief. Wearing the clip all day was like switching seats on the bus. It was like inching out into another world one tiny step at a time.

CHAPTER FIFTEEN

What surprised Figgrotten was how the whole town turned up for Alvin's memorial service that Saturday. There were cars parked all along Main Street, and when she and her family walked into the library, there was barely room for them. The place was mobbed.

"Oh boy," Figgrotten's dad said. "We should have come earlier. Who knew there'd be so many people here?"

The screen up at the front of the big main room, where they showed movies sometimes, was pulled down, and there was a slide show going, with photographs of Alvin. Figgrotten had been distracted by all the people until then, but once she saw Alvin it came back to her why she was there. This was about him.

She made her way up to the front of the crowd by ducking and turning sideways and at one point almost crawling. Finally, when she was at the front, she stood there in her brown coat looking up at the photos. There was a picture of him as a younger man (not that young, actually), wearing hiking boots and holding a walking stick. He had a bandanna wrapped around his head and he was smiling at the camera. There was a picture of him standing in front of the library with a book in his hands. But her favorite picture of all was of him sitting behind the wheel of the school bus, his Greek fisherman's hat on and his hand on the lever of the door like he was about to close it. And the best part of this picture was that his eyes were looking up into the rearview mirror and it seemed he was in the middle of saying something to the kids behind him. Figgrotten stood looking at the pictures as they flicked by, waiting for the bus one to come back again.

She'd left her family by the door, but now, suddenly, she realized that Christinia had also made her way to the front and was standing next to her. And then, when she looked again, there was Ben, standing on the other side of her, so she was between the two of them. Ben was wearing a sports jacket and his hair was combed, which made him look awkward and funny. Somehow this made Figgrotten like him even more. He glanced over at Christinia and said, "Hey," and they all looked up at the photos. There was music playing in the background. Jazzy music with horns. Figgrotten had never known about Alvin's taste in music, but somehow this seemed right.

After a few minutes the head librarian, Madeleine Stroble, got up on the little stand that had been put there and cleared her throat delicately into the microphone. Immediately the crowd became quiet.

"Welcome, everyone, to this celebration, a true celebration, of the life of Alvin Turkson, friend to so many, as is apparent by the size of this crowd. In the spirit of Alvin's inclusive nature, we ask anyone who would like to get up and say a few words to please do so."

Mrs. Stroble stepped off the little stand and someone named Martha Friedman, who seemed downright unsteady, slowly climbed up. She had to have been at least eighty years old.

When she began to speak, the microphone made a horrible screaming noise and needed to be adjusted by a man who seemed to be in charge of the electronics.

Figgrotten caught Ben and Christinia smiling at each other over this.

"Alvin," Mrs. Friedman began in a croaky old voice, "was a friend of mine for forty-eight years. So I knew him pretty well. And I will tell you one thing about him that you all know: He had a heart of pure gold. He was kind to the core, and because of it I will miss him each day."

She reached into the pocket of her pink wool jacket and pulled out a lump of tissues and blew her nose directly and loudly into the microphone. Figgrotten heard a tiny snort next to her and saw that Ben was trying to contain his laughter, and then she saw that Christinia was also trying not to laugh, which made Figgrotten have to bite her own lip to hold back her own giggles.

The next person up on the stand was Alvin's boss at the bus company, a skinny, nervous type who kept wiping his perspiring brow with a handkerchief and who talked about what a dedicated employee Alvin had been for thirty-four years.

"Day in, day out, he was dependable."

Then Mrs. Flynn, the principal, stood up in her same tweedy suit and blue eye shadow and spoke about Alvin. But Figgrotten could tell she hadn't truly known

Alvin the way the other people did. Mrs. Flynn kept up a little of her coldness throughout her speech.

After this, two other old friends got up and told stories about him. One woman talked about Alvin's love of reading, and the other, a very tall, skinny man with a scraggly beard and a ponytail, spoke about a time when they'd gone hiking in the White Mountains of New Hampshire and Alvin had insisted on sitting on top of a mountain during a torrential thunderstorm.

"He said he wanted to feel it," the man said. "I said, 'But if you're dead, you won't feel anything.' At which point he yelled at me and said if I was going to start worrying about dying, then we might as well have stayed home!"

People laughed as the tall skinny man stepped down and walked back into the crowd.

Then no one walked up and there was a long pause. Figgrotten glanced around. She figured the memorial was now over, but everyone was still very quiet. She had the feeling every single person there was thinking about Alvin and feeling the way she did. Sad. So sad.

But then, suddenly, when people started to murmur a little and move around like they were going to leave, Christinia took in a big breath next to Figgrotten and stepped up to the front. Everyone immediately grew quiet again.

Figgrotten froze and her mouth dropped open. Her sister was truly the last person on earth she would have thought would go up there. Indeed, she looked more scared than Figgrotten had ever seen her look. She climbed the steps and took another big breath and then she began to speak. Her voice, at first a little shaky, grew stronger after a second and she stood up straighter.

"Alvin was a friend to all the kids who rode on our bus. But . . ." Christina paused for a second here, then started up again: "But Alvin had a special friendship with my sister, Frances."

At this point, Figgrotten had that terrible feeling in her throat and around her eyes that meant she was going to start crying.

"Everyone knew it too. Frances was Alvin's really great friend," Christinia continued. "They talked every day on the way to school and on the way home. They talked about a lot of things too. We could hear them talking about nature and books. And just life. Lots about life."

Figgrotten was staring at her sister, with her long shining hair and her dark brown eyes. Ben, who was still standing beside Figgrotten, seemed to have moved closer to her, and she could feel that his shoulder was nearly touching hers. She almost had the feeling it was as if he had thrown an arm around her while Christinia spoke.

"You see, Alvin understood and appreciated Frances. Because the fact is, she's a pretty cool person. And he knew it. I mean, he liked everyone. But he really, really loved my sister." Christinia's voice here wobbled suddenly and she paused, then went on. "Because the thing is, he wasn't exactly a teacher, but he *was* a teacher. Alvin was always teaching us how to act because of how he acted. How to listen and be kind to each other and be accepting of each other. And, well, I'll never forget him. And I miss him a lot already."

Then she stopped talking and walked down and came over and stood next to Figgrotten. The crowd was very quiet and a few people could be heard sniffling. But Figgrotten kept her eyes on the floor and didn't look at Christinia. She was frozen. But she was breathing. In and out and in and out. This was to keep from crying. If she was going to cry, it was surely not here, not now, not with Ben standing right next to her.

She stayed quiet too. All the way home in the car, she looked out the window, and then when she went up to the rocks, she stayed very quiet. Quiet as she put the bread out and whistled and watched as the crows flew down to eat the meal they now seemed to depend on.

That night when she got into bed, she lay in the dark with her eyes open. She kept going over what Christinia had said. *"She's a pretty cool person."* She had actually said it up there in front of everyone. And it had worked. It was like Christinia had reached inside her and moved the concrete block that had been so unbudgeable. It was an apology, and the result, Figgrotten could feel, was forgiveness.

After a while she turned on her flashlight and directed the beam around her room. The propped-up branches, the poster of Lucy's bones, the bird feathers she had found over the years that she had scotch-taped up to the wall. There were seventeen of them. Blue jay feathers. Crow feathers. Several gray feathers with a little yellow on them, probably from flycatchers. A huge turkey feather. A striped feather from a hawk and one perfect red feather from a cardinal. She had found each one on the ground, and each time she had found one it had given her the same thrill. As if someone had left her a gift.

"The natural world is filled with wonders, Miss Pauley, and to sit up there in that rock world and be an observer of it all . . . well . . . what a terrific thing that is."

Right there and then, Alvin's voice, his face, his hat, his skinny arms coming out of his short-sleeved button-down checkered shirt, his small dark eyes—suddenly everything about him came to her in perfect clarity. *Oh, Alvin,* she thought. And with this, the dreadful ache came up through her, it pushed through her throat, and finally little streams of tears began to trickle out of her eyes. And this time she just let them go. She couldn't stop them anymore. She would never ever see him again. It was just the absolute bare bones of the truth, and she could no longer not face it. She could no longer push away the sadness. She rolled her face into her pillow and a little sob came from somewhere deep within her. It was almost like a little freed bird that had been caught somewhere. And then, as she predicted, the crying began and it didn't stop for a long time. She sobbed and kept sobbing into her pillow. But then, finally, she was done and she turned onto her back and lay breathing in hiccuppy, stuttery breaths. She was horribly sad still, but now it was not locked inside her and she felt peaceful in a way she had not felt in a long, long time.

"Were you married ever, Alvin?" she'd asked him one afternoon this past fall.

"No, not officially. But yes, I was married in every other sense of the word to a wonderful woman for forty-seven years."

"What was her name?"

"Sylvia," Alvin said, and then he shook his head. And Figgrotten could tell he was remembering. "But I only called her sweetheart."

"Where is she now?" Figgrotten asked.

"Oh, Miss Pauley, she's here and there and she's everywhere. In the air, she is." Alvin then took his hand off the steering wheel and made a sweeping motion out in front of him.

Figgrotten was remembering this when she fell asleep. And she realized she felt it too. Alvin *was* here. He was there. He was everywhere now.

CHAPTER SIXTEEN

The following week Figgrotten took Christinia's suggestion and began wearing two hair clips, one on each side of her head. She found the second one next to her toothbrush in the bathroom, and she was pretty sure Christinia had left it there for her. Wearing her hair like this made her look around a bit to see if anyone noticed, and it did seem that more people glanced at her and these glances made her feel like she was a part of things in a way she hadn't quite felt before.

The only problem with her new hair was that wearing a hat kind of ruined it. So, suddenly, she was going out to the bus stop in the mornings hatless, the bitter wind drilling into her ears. And for the first time she understood why Christinia didn't dress right for the cold.

Starting on Monday Christinia came out and waited for the bus beside Figgrotten. "You realize you're lucky you have curly hair, right?" she told her.

Figgrotten shook her head. "Um, no. Not lucky."

"Yes. And I read that if you don't wash your hair too much and then don't brush it ever, you'll get really nice curls. Just let it dry naturally." Christinia paused, then sort of blurted out, "And also, Frances, I'm sorry I made up that story about telling my friends you were adopted. I didn't do that. I'm sorry that I told you that."

When Figgrotten heard this, she held back from letting herself get teary. She'd suffered needlessly for something that didn't even happen. But finally she shrugged. She was so used to not speaking to Christinia that speaking felt downright awkward. Then finally she said, "Okay. I'm glad you didn't say it."

From her new seat nearer to the back, Figgrotten could observe the other riders in a way she hadn't been able to when she sat in the front behind Alvin. Now she could not only look at the back of Ben's and Christinia's heads, she could also see everyone else except for the few behind her. But she mostly found she was focused on James. He sat in the most slumped-down position of all, his head hanging forward over his book. While this had annoyed Figgrotten to begin with, now it just made her feel bad. She knew her yelling in the class that day had probably just made him all the more lonely and miserable, and now every time she saw him it bothered her. Being mean like that had made a kind of bruise inside herself that wasn't going away. In fact it seemed to be getting worse.

Behind her in the backseat, she also knew, was Becky Moss, who used to be Christinia's friend. She wasn't sure whether Ben's moving out of the seat to sit with Christinia that first time had been what Becky deserved. Someday, if she and Christinia ever got to be close enough again, she might ask her this. There were certain things she didn't quite understand still. Who was friends with who, who wasn't, why groups of kids were together for a while, then not together. Why those two bully girls walked around needing to be mean. But it occupied a lot of her thinking now. Especially without Alvin there to talk about bigger, deeper things.

All she did know was that having Fiona now as her friend changed just about everything. It made her feel stronger to always have someone by her side and to share secrets and jokes with her. They gave each other looks throughout each class. About having another math quiz, about being bored, and about counting down the minutes until they were released for recess. They made scrunched-up faces, or rolled their eyes, or raised their eyebrows. Fiona was smart about things in a way Figgrotten had never known before. She had figured people's personalities out and understood the way certain people interacted with other people. "Those girls are cliquey," she'd say, pointing at a group of girls whispering together at the picnic table.

"They are?" Figgrotten would look at them and narrow her eyes a bit. In fact, Fiona was kind of like an anthropologist too! Plus she was funny. She made up names for different people, referring to Mr. Stanley as "Stan the Man." And Gordie Horen was "Gordon Boring."

For the past couple of days, Figgrotten and Fiona had gone into the bathroom together during recess and stood in front of the mirror and rearranged their hair. Fiona had long brown hair that hung down to her shoulders, but she didn't do much with it. She just let it droop. Figgrotten pointed out to her that when she pulled it back, you could really see her pretty eyes and that the blue of them seemed even bluer. "Ick," Fiona said, and made a face at herself in the mirror. Figgrotten knew the feeling. While she'd never thought much about her own looks before, now, most of the time when she looked in the mirror, the same thought went through her head. *Ick*. But once in a while, if she turned this way and that way, and if the light was a certain way, she thought that maybe it wasn't totally ick. She remembered spying on her sister staring at herself in the mirror all those times, and she realized, sure enough, as her mom had predicted, now she seemed to be doing it too.

It was when she and Fiona were stepping out of the girls' room that Wednesday that Figgrotten caught sight of James coming from the school library with a book in his hands. He looked like he always looked, unhappy, walking with his head down so that his hair hung around his face. Figgrotten suddenly stopped and waited for him to get close to her, then she said, "Hi, James," in a super-cheerful casual voice. Like it was something she always did.

James looked up, startled, and then said, "Oh. Um. Hi." And he paused for a second, not quite knowing what he was supposed to do next; then he continued past.

Once he had turned and gone outside, Fiona grabbed

Figgrotten and said, "Oh wow! Wow! Why did you say hi to *him*?"

Figgrotten shrugged. "I don't know. He seems kind of lonely."

"But he's such a smarty-pants," Fiona said.

And Figgrotten shrugged. "Yeah, that's for sure."

But she didn't tell Fiona that saying hi to James was something that she needed to do to make up for screaming at him. Besides, there was something she had started to see in him. And she was pretty sure it was plain old loneliness. And she now was starting to know, even with Alvin as her best friend, she had been a little lonely too for a long time.

The thing that surprised her was how just saying hi to James made her feel like a weight had been lifted off of *her*. And there was that little bridge again that went right up between her and him. And now she knew she could cross over.

That same afternoon, Fiona went over to Figgrotten's house for the first time. They were to spend the afternoon together and Fiona's mom was picking her up after dinner. As excited as Figgrotten was about having her, she was also nervous. She was mostly worried about what Fiona would think of her bedroom.

"Prepare yourself," Figgrotten said as they climbed the stairs after eating a snack in the kitchen.

"How come?"

"Oh," Figgrotten said with a shrug, "I think you'll see."

Figgrotten swung open the door to her room and Fiona stepped inside. "Whoa," Fiona said quietly. Then, "Holy moly." She stood in the middle of the room with her hands hanging at her sides and her mouth open, and very slowly she turned, looking around, her eyes taking in the Lucy poster, the branches, the taped feathers, the new photos of Gandhi and Mead that Figgrotten had found on the Internet, printed out, and taped next to her bed.

Figgrotten was standing in the doorway, biting her lower lip. She figured this could very well be the straw that broke the camel's back. She knew Fiona might see all the branches and just think, *Too weird.* After all, Fiona's room was pink. Pink. Pink and more pink.

"Um," Figgrotten said. "Yeah, I realize it's a bit odd in here."

Figgrotten's voice seemed to snap Fiona back into the moment and she spun around with her eyes wide open and sort of shrieked with laughter. "Yeah, that's for sure! It's hysterical. I love it!" Then the laughing started and the two of them collapsed on the bed, trying to get hold of themselves. Once Fiona had pulled herself together, she wiped away the tears that were rolling down her face and began asking Figgrotten about everything. The feathers, the posters, the branches, her books.

"Where do you play music from?" she asked.

"I don't really listen to music," Figgrotten said, causing another eruption of hysterics, which ended only when there was a knock on the door and Christinia stepped into the room. Fiona immediately grew quiet and shy.

"What's so funny?" Christinia asked. "Anyway, if you guys want, I'll give you makeovers later."

Fiona's eyes widened again. "Oh boy, that would be so cool," she said.

There was a time when Christinia's offer would have irritated Figgrotten, but now, somehow, she welcomed it. After all, Fiona did have a very pink bedroom, so adding some girly stuff to the afternoon was probably a good idea.

It was another frigid-cold day, so a little while later, when Figgrotten took Fiona up onto the rocks, Fiona's teeth were chattering. But she sat in the little rock chair and looked all around.

"Oh," she said, quietly shivering, "this is so pretty."

"I sort of live up here," Figgrotten said. "I mean, I'm up here like *all* the time."

"I'd be here all the time too. It's like an outdoor house."

"Exactly," Figgrotten said. Then she explained about whistling for the crows.

"Do they come when you whistle?" Fiona asked.

"Well, honestly, they are here *before* I whistle. In fact, they're always pretty much around now. You see?" Figgrotten pointed up to the trees behind her. "There they are!"

Fiona looked up. "Oh, cool!" she said. Then she dropped her head back farther and stared into the sky and took a big breath. "Wow, isn't it just so weird to look out into space and think it goes on forever? I can't even think about it at all."

"Yeah." Figgrotten was now looking up too. She was thinking about Alvin telling her about the discovery of the new planet. "I mean, we're not even the size of a speck of dust in comparison to how big everything is."

"Nope." Fiona put her hands up to the sides of her head. "Can't think about it. Brain too small!"

They both laughed.

They weren't up on the rocks for long because of the cold and because, really, there wasn't much to do up there together. In fact, for the first time, when Fiona was with her, the rocks were not as interesting to Figgrotten.

They went into the house and made chocolate chip cookies, which caused several bouts of hysterics. Especially when they realized Figgrotten had accidentally set the oven temp to 450 degrees instead of 350 degrees and the first batch came out smoking and black and then set the smoke detector in the kitchen off. Figgrotten melted onto the floor at one point and almost peed in her pants, and later, after Fiona went home, she realized her stomach muscles hurt like crazy from so much laughing and everything seemed a bit dull now that she was alone.

CHAPTER SEVENTEEN

Christinia's favorite place in the entire world was the Shanoosik Mall. So when the three of them—Figgrotten, her mom, and her sister—stepped into the vast echoing building, Christinia almost levitated off the floor with excitement.

She started talking very fast and broke into a full run, pointing at different stores she wanted to go into. Mrs. Pauley took a deep breath and told Christinia to cool her jets. "Limited funds," she sighed. "So, limited fun."

"Oh, Mom, you always say that!" Christinia moaned.

"Okay, okay," their mom said. "You lead the way. We'll let you shop for the first leg of this."

Figgrotten, already sweating under her brown wool coat, was wishing she'd been allowed to stay home and spend the day up on the rocks. It was cold and clear and beautiful outside. But the fact was she had to go, as all three pairs of her shoes were getting too small for her and it had become a real problem. Even now, as she followed Christinia into a store that had deafeningly loud music and blinking lights, her toes were pressed up against the front of her sneakers and they were starting to hurt.

Christinia was moving through the racks at lightning speed, and Figgrotten and her mom exchanged glances. But then Figgrotten's mom shrugged and started poking through the racks of clothes as well. Figgrotten had her hands clasped behind her back and she walked slowly around the store. Stores always made her feel super hot and weak-tired. For someone who never had taken a nap her entire life, Figgrotten always wanted one when she was in any kind of clothing store. She yawned and looked around and then something caught her eye and she went up to one of the racks and studied what turned out to be a large brown puffy coat with a fake-fur hood. It reminded her of the jacket she'd seen in the old photos of Robert Peary, the guy who had first explored the North Pole. Figgrotten unbuttoned her wool coat, placed it carefully on the floor by her feet, and slipped into the puffy coat, and instantaneously she knew it was for her. It was lightweight but warm. In fact, it reminded her of her beloved sleeping bag, which was one of her most prized possessions. She pulled the hood up over her head and cinched it around her face so just her nose was exposed, then she walked over to the full-length mirror and looked at herself.

She turned to each side, then stood facing herself.

"Hey, that's pretty cool," Christinia said. "I mean, you can't wear the hood up like that unless you're completely alone, but other than that, it looks kind of good. Those coats are in now."

"Plus it fits you, unlike your old coat." Her mom was now looking at her as well.

Figgrotten looked over at her wool coat on the floor and felt a surge of sadness. The coat was a friend to her.

"If I get this, I won't have to give up my old coat, will I, Mom?" she asked.

Christinia and her mom chuckled at this. "Obviously you can keep it," her mom said.

Figgrotten walked over and picked it up and gave it a reassuring hug, but she didn't take off the new coat and each time she caught a glance of herself in a mirror she felt excited. The way she'd felt when she put the clip into her hair. It was different and new and it looked good. Almost pretty.

Things didn't go as smoothly in the shoe store, however. The shoes Figgrotten chose were what Christinia referred to as "man shoes." And she became enraged at one point about them.

But Figgrotten didn't give a hoot. The shoes were a cross between a sneaker and a hiking boot, and they had massive treads that she imagined would cling to the rocks so perfectly she wouldn't have to use her hands going up and down.

"But they don't look good!" Christinia practically wailed.

"So!" Figgrotten snapped. "They feel good. It's not all about looking good, you know."

"Ugh," Christinia said, and turned and walked out of the store.

But Figgrotten got the shoes anyway, and when they sat down for slices of pizza in the food court, she had on both her new coat and her new shoes, and she was beginning, for the first time, to understand why the mall was sort of okay. Mrs. Pauley was going over her list of things they still needed to get when Christinia suddenly sat up and said, "Hey, look, there's Mr. Stanley!"

And sure enough, there he was, standing out in front of Barnes and Noble, looking into the window. Figgrotten set her pizza down. She was thinking she'd run over to him and say hi, but she hesitated. She felt a little familiar stab about him. He looked so alone there, on a Saturday, at the mall. But then, just as she was thinking this, a man came out of the store and it was clear that Mr. Stanley had been waiting for him. They spoke to each other and laughed and walked on.

Figgrotten now had forgotten about her pizza. There was something about the way the two of them walked together, a kind of familiarity with each other, that made her suddenly think. She glanced over at Christinia and her mom and they both looked the same way.

"Oh wow." Christinia sat back in her chair. "I think Mr. Stanley maybe has a boyfriend! *Cool!*" she said.

"You know, it's possible," Figgrotten's mom said.

But Figgrotten hadn't moved. Her mind was all topsy-turvy, as a new thought had flown in. Maybe Mr. Stanley was gay. She knew about people being gay from her Life Studies class, but she'd never known anyone who was, in fact, gay.

"Frances," her mom was saying. "Honey, there are many people who are gay. You know that, right?"

"I just had no idea," Figgrotten said. "I'm just so . . ." She paused and looked at her mom. "I'm just so relieved he's not alone. I mean, maybe that was his husband."

Christinia made a soft noise and Figgrotten turned and saw her sister's eyes had teeny-tiny tears swimming around the edges. Christinia leaned over and threw both her arms around her sister and sniffed.

"Aww, that's so nice," Christinia said softly.

Thinking that Mr. Stanley might be gay made Figgrotten like and respect him even more than she had before. Now, not only was he smart, he was courageous because he was being himself. She knew firsthand this was never easy. It was nothing she hadn't known already about him, but this just proved it even more.

Figgrotten's mom told her she thought it might be better not to tell everyone that Mr. Stanley had a boyfriend. "Sad to say, people can be unkind."

"The word is also *prejudiced,*" Christinia said through a bite of pizza.

Figgrotten didn't need to be told any of this. She knew about unkindness. The two girls making the gagging sound at her in the bathroom came into her mind. And, horribly, her yelling at James was another example. Yes, she thought, she knew all about that sort of thing.

CHAPTER EIGHTEEN

Figgrotten stood in her new coat and big clodhopper "man shoes" in the cold air. Off in the distance she could hear the bus approaching, and the sound of it roaring and grinding made her heart sink yet again. These were just more reminders that Alvin was no longer at the wheel. She'd found out that the new bus driver's name was Kevin Plank, and she'd also found out that he worked at the service station in town during the day when he wasn't driving the bus. That explained why his hands were so black and greasy-looking.

Figgrotten decided she would never get used to him.

He was the complete opposite kind of human being from Alvin. Alvin: interesting, smart, kind. Kevin: boring, dumb, mean. Well, she thought, to be honest, he wasn't exactly mean; he was just a dull person who drove badly and sat expressionless under his orange hunting hat. And the fact that he'd taken Alvin's place made her unable not to hate him.

As the bus pulled up with a dreadful shudder, Figgrotten stood feeling disgusted, then climbed on without even looking at him. She plopped into her seat and took the position of most of the kids—slumped, staring out the window, watching the town go past. She knew the route so well she could ride with her eyes shut and still somehow know exactly where they were: whose house they were passing, which pothole they were about to hit. For years the ride had been the highlight of her day, but now it was dull and endless and painful.

Today when they drove out of town and up onto Prunick Ridge Road, the bus started shuddering in a whole new way; then, suddenly, after a kind of cough followed by a loud high-pitched noise, the thing died right in the middle of the road. Figgrotten sat up and fixed her eyes on the orange hunting hat. It didn't move for a minute. It just sat there. Then it leaned forward and the orange hat's hand turned the key, but there was absolutely nothing coming from the engine but a soft clicking noise. Then silence. Then a loud cheer from the kids in the backseat. "Woooo-hooo!" one of them hollered. "Stranded!"

But Figgrotten had leaned forward and was watching Kevin. He was moving just as slowly as ever, it seemed. He leaned to the side and opened the door, then stood up and stepped down off the bus. She'd never seen him standing and it was a bit of a shocker. He didn't seem to unfold normally. He was almost as short standing as he was sitting.

The hood of the bus opened and there were small squeaky noises, then some clanging, then silence. Then the orange hat came back up the steps, sat down, paused, turned the key again. This time there was a soft whining noise, then the same dead click. The hat went back down the steps with what looked like a toolbox in his hands this time, and for five minutes there was all sorts of banging and clanging. Then back up the steps the hat came. It sat down, leaned forward, turned the key, and after a few whines the engine bloomed into a roar and it was running.

"Awwww," the kids in the back groaned with disappointment. "Boooo!"

But Figgrotten was watching Kevin's face in his rearview mirror. He sat back in his seat for a second and then hit the steering wheel gently with both hands in a moment of triumph. He then got out and shut the hood, and when he climbed back on, Figgrotten saw him trying to contain his own pleased smile.

The bus was clearly still not working right as they made their way slowly to school. It made a loud roaring noise the entire way, and Kevin seemed to drive extra carefully and slowly.

"Every single person has one of these," Alvin had said, pounding on his chest, right over his heart. Figgrotten stared out the window and heard Alvin's voice. He'd told her that for a reason.

The night before, Figgrotten had pulled out her journal and was turning back through the pages when the little slip of paper with Alvin's handwriting had drifted out. She'd put it there, the Gandhi quote that she'd never really understood. But now she held it, staring at Alvin's rickety writing. "An eye for an eye only ends up making the whole world blind." She read the sentence out loud and finally she began to understand what it meant. It was about how getting even with people didn't work. And there it was again, an example of a vicious cycle.

She wondered if she hadn't tried to get even with some people.

And when she fell asleep, it was slowly dawning on her that yes. Yes. She had done exactly this.

When they finally pulled up in front of the school, Figgrotten lingered in her seat while everyone else got off the bus. She pretended she was gathering her stuff together even though it was already gathered. Finally she stood up and came down the aisle and stopped at the top step.

"Thanks for fixing the bus. You sure are a good mechanic," she said, and just before she stepped down off the bus, she saw him smile a little and nod; then his face got super red. Just like hers.

He wasn't stupid after all.

He was just horribly shy.

Mr. Stanley came into the room that morning dressed in his usual snappy outfit. Purple vest, gray tie, button-down blue shirt. And his shiny brown shoes that made a wonderful clean clicking noise as he walked.

"Good morning, class!" he said, and as always he sounded excited. "Today is a very special day. Today we will spend the morning discussing a person named

Lucy. She is the oldest person in the world. And she's about this tall and she grew up in Africa. Now, tell me, do any of you know who I might be talking about? Does anyone here know who Lucy is?"

Mr. Stanley turned toward the blackboard and wrote the word LUCY across it in big capital letters.

Figgrotten glanced around and saw that no hands had gone up. Even James sat thinking but clearly didn't know the answer.

Figgrotten put her hand up as gently as possible.

Mr. Stanley turned, walked over to her, folded his arms across his chest, and smiled down at her. "Frances, please tell us who she is."

Figgrotten looked at all her classmates. She could really go on about Lucy. She could tell everyone that she was found in 1974, and that an archaeologist named Donald Johanson had found her and that the song "Lucy in the Sky with Diamonds" by the Beatles was playing when they discovered her and that is why they called her Lucy, and they dug up several hundred fragments of her bones, and she had stood three feet seven inches tall and she had weighed sixty-four pounds. And lots of other things.

But instead Figgrotten just said, "She's one of the oldest skeletons of a person ever found." She paused and then said, "So she's like everyone's great-great-great-great-aunt. She's amazing."

And when she looked up, Mr. Stanley was still standing there smiling at her, but his head had tilted ever so slightly to one side and he seemed lost in thought.

He let out a little breath, then said, "Well, it's good to know there is someone else who feels the way I do about her. Indeed, she was and is amazing. Today we will talk all about her."

Figgrotten tried to contain her own smile. Mr. Stanley remained the world's greatest teacher and the look he had given made her know he still appreciated her. Even if James knew more of the answers than she did.

That day at recess it was sunny out and finally slightly warmer. Fiona and Figgrotten walked out to the rock at the far side of the playground and leaned against it. Fiona tilted her head back and closed her eyes. "I'm getting a tan. My mom said I look pale as a cadaver."

But Figgrotten was watching James. As usual he sat with his back against the wall, reading his book. "Never forget that everyone needs plenty of understanding. Just as you do. And as do I. People are very different, but they are very, very similar too," Alvin had said.

Reaching out to Kevin on the bus had confirmed there was one more thing that she had to do. Alvin would have wanted her to.

Figgrotten told Fiona to hang on for a second and she walked over to where James was sitting.

"Hey," she said to him. He looked up at her and squinted, as the sun was behind her. "You know, no one answered any questions except for me before you came into the class."

James looked both confused and scared. "Oh, um," he said, clearly not knowing how to respond to Figgrotten.

"So, you know, I wasn't used to it."

"Used to what?"

"Used to having someone else who knew stuff."

"Oh . . . I . . . um . . . oh, but you know more stuff than I do. Like that old skeleton . . . ," James said, which surprised her.

"Her name is Lucy." Figgrotten smiled. "And yeah, but no, you know a lot more."

"I don't think—" he started to say.

But she didn't let him finish. "Anyway, I'm really sorry I yelled that time. I was having a terrible week and I'm sorry I took it out on you."

"Oh," James said. "Well . . . I . . . don't . . ."

"So anyway, can you please tell me what's so interesting about that book you're reading?"

James was still looking up at her. "My . . . ?"

"The book, what's the book?" Figgrotten pointed.

"Oh." James looked down at the book in his lap and shut it and held it out to Figgrotten. She took it and read the title, *Watership Down.* There was a rabbit on the front.

"It's about a bunch of rabbits," James said. "But, well, it's not really about that. It's sort of—well, it's kind of weird. But I've read it three times."

Figgrotten handed him back the book. "Oh" was all she could think to say. Somehow it was a relief it was a book about a bunch of rabbits and not about something scientific that she would never be able to understand. And at least there was an outdoor element to it.

She was looking down at him now and he was looking up at her. "Well." She shrugged. "Okay, now I know. I don't read many books like that. I read the encyclopedia mostly. But maybe I'll try it sometime. Anyway, if you want to come over and hang around with me and Fiona, you can."

"Oh." His mouth was hanging open a bit and he was still looking up at her. "Oh, okay."

And to Figgrotten's surprise, he shut his book immediately and stood up and followed her over to the rock. Fiona looked super confused at first, but then Figgrotten asked James after a couple of awkward moments, "Have you ever played Snapshot?"

He shook his head. "I don't think so."

"You wanna play?"

He shrugged again. "Not really, but I guess, okay."

For some reason this struck Fiona as funny, and the chipmunk laugh swooped out and up. And Figgrotten saw James's startled expression at first, then she saw the laugh break something in him and he started chuckling too.

"Okay, here's what we do," she said. "We all close our eyes for a second, then we open them and look around, then we close them again, and turn around. Then we ask questions and try to see who can remember what. Like 'What color is so-and-so's shirt?' Or 'What game were the kids by the picnic table playing?' You get it?"

"Yeah, I guess," James said, though he sounded baffled.

"Okay, ready? Close your eyes. Keep them closed. Okay, open them and look. Look . . . One. Two. Three. Okay, close them and turn around."

Figgrotten opened her eyes and saw that both Fiona and James had turned around and were looking at her.

"Okay, so, what color pants is, um, Megan wearing today?"

James said, "Wait, who's Megan?"

At which point Fiona totally lost it. Then it caught on and they all were trying to contain themselves.

"Okay, let's try it again."

They went through the same process and this time Figgrotten's question was, "Okay, what was Marshall doing just now?"

This time James started to laugh.

"What's so funny?"

"Who's Marshall?" he said.

"Awkward!" Fiona said, which made them all, once again, lose it.

On the bus on the way home that day, Figgrotten sat once again looking at the back of James's head. He was of course back to looking down into his rabbit book. While they were out by the rock laughing together, she'd finally seen it. She hadn't seen it before but there was something about James's laugh and the way he stood that made the word come into her head. *Cute.* And once that word appeared, she knew she'd had another thought-wrencher, because everything shifted a little, once again, from this one little thought.

CHAPTER NINETEEN

That Thursday there was an early dismissal because another storm was in the forecast. And sure enough, the snow had started falling before the bus dropped her and Christinia off in front of the house. There was a note on the kitchen table from their mom, who had run out to the grocery store. So Figgrotten and Christinia sat down at the kitchen table together and opened their lunch boxes.

As she did every day, Figgrotten ate her cookies first and then her carrot sticks and then her sandwich.

"Cookies are the dessert," Christinia said through a mouthful of sandwich.

Figgrotten shrugged. "Sandwich is my dessert."

Her sister sighed. "I guess I should be used to it at this point."

"Yup." Figgrotten smiled and bit into a carrot stick. "You should."

"Wanna watch TV?"

"Can't. Have to feed the crows."

Christinia rolled her eyes and shook her head. "In the storm?"

Figgrotten shrugged and slipped her jacket on.

"Well, Ben says you're an original," Christinia said, then tipped her head back and took a drink from her water bottle. Then she put the bottle down and burped softly.

"He said that?" Figgrotten stood frozen at the mention of Ben's name.

"Yup. But I told him I already figured that out on my own." She smiled at Figgrotten after saying this.

Figgrotten wanted to ask what else Ben had said about her, but she thought this might reveal that she liked him. So instead she pulled her massive hood up over her head and looked at Christinia through the narrow tunnel-like opening. "Peary!" she hissed.

"What?" Christinia stared at her.

"He was a famous explorer. . . . Oh, never mind."

Figgrotten grabbed the bag of bread crusts her mom had left and went out the door. The fact that Ben had said this about her made her happy.

Up on the rocks that day in her massive new jacket and her "man shoes," Figgrotten sat in the snowstorm as warm and comfortable as could be. The snow was coming down straight and soft and silent, and quickly it began to cover everything. Even the bread she put down for the crows was now white with it. Figgrotten stood up and pulled her hood off her head for a minute and whistled a second time. Then she pulled it back on and sat down, and before she could think, when she was least expecting it, one of the crows came out of nowhere and landed on her rock, inches from where she was sitting. She could have reached out and stroked his shining black head. But she froze and held her breath and stared at the bird. Her heart was whomping hard in her chest. She almost felt as though she was dreaming, but she wasn't. The crow was right there. Right next to her.

The bird didn't seem to notice her. It sat tilting its head one way and then the other, then suddenly it rocked back and cawed so loudly that Figgrotten jumped a little inside her coat. But then she kept still even as the three other birds dropped down to the ledge below, where the bread was, and began picking at it. Only when the crow sitting beside her flew down to join them did she let out a big breath and relax a little. She wondered if her new brown coat with the fur-lined hood was the reason the bird had sat so close to her. Was it possible the crow hadn't realized she was a human? Unlikely, she thought, seeing that crows were so smart.

Somewhere in the back of her mind, she had imagined her experiment would lead to her whistling all four crows straight down to her. She'd even pictured them landing on her shoulders or head. But she pretty much knew that wasn't going to happen now. That was the thing about wildlife. It really was wild. And that was what she loved about it. But at the same time, her experiment hadn't been a complete bust. She knew the crows knew her and trusted her now. In fact, maybe they had run their own experiment by having the one land next to her, and the results, with her sitting so quiet and still, were just as they had hoped.

Later, once the birds had devoured the crusts and had flown up into the pines, Figgrotten climbed down off the rocks and went into the house. She shook off the snow that covered her and hung up her coat in the kitchen.

"A crow landed right next to me," she said to Christinia, who was watching a music video on TV.

"It what?"

"This crow landed right next to me on the rock!" Figgrotten said, shouting a little above the music.

Christinia turned and looked at her and blinked. "Cool," she said, then turned back to the TV.

Figgrotten went up to her room and sat down on the floor. She looked around at her posters and feathers and branches. Her sister's reaction to the crow was to be expected. Her "rock world," as Alvin used to call it, was just that. *Her* world. Just like the card she had tacked on her door bearing the name Figgrotten. Though Christinia had crumpled it up that time, Figgrotten had smoothed it out and put it inside the first page of her journal. Not exactly hidden, but not where everyone had to see it either. She could hang on to who she was and still be part of the world, which she could now feel tugging at her. It came as a little longing to cross paths with Ben in the hallway, a longing to hear Fiona's chipmunk laugh, and even as a pull to go sit with her sister in front of the TV.

She looked up at her poster of Lucy and remembered Christinia telling her it was creepy to have it up there, and suddenly she thought maybe it *was* a bit creepy. Maybe she should take it down. She sat for a long time staring at all the different bones. Each one a spectacular find. But to have come across the little skull? The archaeologists on the dig must have gone berserk when they found it. This thought made her happy and she stood up and walked over to the poster, and instead of taking it down, she planted a kiss on the top of Lucy's skull.

Maybe, she thought, the branches should go. After all, they were dead and they were sort of making a big mess of things. But she needed to think about it first.

She then went downstairs and plopped onto the couch next to her sister.

"Can't we watch a show about something real?" Figgrotten asked.

"Nope," Christinia said. "We're watching this."

The fact that Christinia said "we're" instead of "I'm" made Figgrotten settle deeper into the sofa and focus on the girl wearing super-short shorts dancing across the screen.

It wasn't her "cup of tea," but as Alvin used to always say, "Don't forget that you're not always there for the tea." She remembered him saying this to her one day last year. He was looking at her in his rearview mirror, smiling. And here Figgrotten was now, not forgetting it. Not forgetting Alvin and all he had given to her. Not ever.

She crossed her legs and focused on the TV screen, but a few moments later she realized her eyes had wandered away from it and she was looking out the window at the white wintery world, the snow drifting down in big, slow, floating flakes.

She imagined being out in the nice cold fresh air, up on her rocks, waiting for the crows to come back, but she stayed right where she was, in the company of her sister, surprised to see her own foot jiggling a little to the beat of music.

ACKNOWLEDGMENTS

Carrie Hannigan and Lee Wade, your support and understanding of Figgrotten were, in turn, support and kindness for me. Each of you, equally, nurtured this book until it stood on its own two feet.

Deep gratitude to the following people for their guidance, friendship, patience, and laughter:

Sara, Sheila, Kari, Nora, Tory, Judith, Michael, Tammy, Elizabeth, Mary Kay, Ellen, Jackie, Valorie, Olive, Eliza, Alex, Marcia, Steph, Jeanne, Katie, Jacque, Gregg, and Gina.

And of course, thank you to my family: Sam, for always being one step ahead of me; Willa, for your insight and your beautiful empathetic heart; and Sandy, lifelong editor, encourager, stabilizer, and best friend.

ABOUT THE AUTHOR

April Stevens is the author of two children's picture books, *Edwin Speaks Up* and *Waking Up Wendell.* Both books received two starred reviews, and *Waking Up Wendell* was named a Bank Street College of Education Best Children's Book of the Year. She is also the author of the acclaimed novel for adults *Angel, Angel.* April lives in Connecticut.